# THE TIME KEEPER

## TRISH ALBRIGHT

ISBN-10: 1938258118

ISBN-13: 978-1-938258-11-4



Cover and book design by

*Hot* DAMN DESIGNS

www.HotDamnDesigns.com

# DEDICATION

To my Readers
Thank you for purchasing this book.
I hope it brings you hours of fun.

Follow me on Twitter and Facebook:
Trish Albright
Or visit my blog at TrishAlbright.com

# BOOKS BY TRISH ALBRIGHT

KEEPERS OF THE LEGACY SERIES
Siren's Song, book 1
Siren's Secret, book 2
Siren's Sanctuary, Coming 2013


The Time Keeper, October 2012

# THE TIME KEEPER

# CHAPTER ONE

*1720 – Greenwich, England*

Avery held her treasured timepiece up to the last remnants of light. Three fifty-nine. In two minutes sunlight would be gone entirely.

In one minute, the game would begin.

Or should she say, continue?

Time played an important role in Avery Hilfington's life. Thirteen years since her father had perished, along with sixteen hundred others in the Royal Navy; six years since Parliament had passed the Longitude Act; four years since…

She lifted the gold chain and slipped the watch under her shirt, secure against her heart, then shivered. The delicate instrument had once comforted her. Now the cold metal merely reminded her that temperatures had dropped steadily all week, winter storms would pick up at sea, and thousands of men would once again be in danger.

*Four years since he'd left.*

She closed her eyes against the memory of that one man—the one who had been her friend and companion for the duration of her life.

The bell tower made its first chime, beginning to mark the evening hour.

For four years he had carefully avoided seeing her. Four years for her to come to terms with her feelings. Four years in which she'd focused solely on solving the problem of longitude.

The last chime sounded four o'clock. Then silence.

She waited.

At four o'clock Dr. Llewellyn would begin evening rounds, then dinner would be served.

Avery slid behind heavy curtains that covered the windows in the hallway, her footsteps soft on the chilled tile, her heart pounding loudly in anticipation of her actions. She reminded herself this was necessary, and reasonably justified. She wasn't breaking into anyone's office who had not already broken into her home.

She recounted milestones in an effort to calm herself and rationalize her actions.

Four years since Luc had gone to sea; one year since Professor Edmond Halley had become Astronomer Royal; six months since she had completed design on the sea watch; one week since the watch had been stolen. Forty-eight hours since she'd discovered the culprit. Three hours since she'd stolen a set of keys. One minute before she would recover what was hers.

It was time.

A knock at the door alerted her. Her recent reconnaissance paid off as the evening nurse fetched the doctor for end of day rounds.

The door closed.

The lock clicked.

Avery tucked her toes behind the heavy curtain and pressed against the frozen glass, hoping the thick folds looked perfectly normal to a passerby.

She heard two sets of footsteps coming closer, the momentum of their gait ruffling the material concealing her. She counted down the ten steps before they would turn the corner. At ten, she darted from her hiding place and put her plan into action.

Her hands trembled slightly as she fumbled to find the right key. An echo of new, heavier footfalls sounded from around the corner.

The key didn't fit. "Damn." She tried the next one.

The footsteps became louder, and despite all her planning, her hands lacked their usual dexterity. She inserted the last key. Click. Avery checked that no one watched as she slipped inside the doctor's suite.

Once inside, she inhaled deeply and gently closed the door, locking it behind her. She waited until the footsteps passed before releasing her breath.

Having recovered her composure, she put her basket of goods on a chair by the coat rack and looked about. A door led to what she guessed was an examination room. In the main room, a full-length human skeleton hung in one corner followed by a wall of medical books. She walked past the form, poking the ribs causing the bones to dangle spookily, an arm reaching out to her.

"Sorry, old fellow. Not here to rescue you."

A large desk was placed in the middle of the room, but it was the table behind the powerful desk that got her attention. Here were items of science and astronomy: a small scope, a globe, a quadrant, an old mariner's astrolabe, and a volume of the late Flamsteed's astronomical observations open to notations on the December sky. In the center of it all was a velvet cloth, spread approximately four feet wide. The contents underneath it were concealed by another velvet cloth.

Avery's hand shook as she ascertained the shape was not of her timepiece. She had an instant premonition this would not end well. Carefully, she removed the velvet— only to suffer paralyzing shock.

Avery did not know an occasion when she wasn't consumed with time. It wasn't a particularly unusual obsession, at least not in Greenwich. Everyone in the town prayed for a solution to longitude, and in the six years since the Longitude Act had passed with the reward of twenty thousand pounds to whomever found the solution, Greenwich had seen its share of kooks, schemes and scams. For Avery, it wasn't about the money. It was about life. Human life. She didn't care that the solution would advance British imperialism, or help fill the coffers of the king. She simply wanted their brave seamen to have a fighting chance at returning home. With better navigation, the accident that had taken her father away could have been prevented.

That's why she had devoted her life to study. That's why she had slaved for four years to find a mechanism to measure time at sea. That's why she nearly exposed herself now with a furious scream of epic proportions.

Instead she choked.

Time did not stand still, as most people would have said. No. Time was in pieces, spread out in parts all over the villain's desk. Horror burned through her chest.

"Bloody, stupid, devious, stealing, miserable bastard."

Years of work lay disassembled and destroyed before her. She didn't know where to begin or what to do next. Anger and hopelessness nearly left her undone. She dragged in her breath, fighting back tears. Nearly undone. She was stronger than this. Years of focus had made her stronger than this.

She could not think about the future. She needed to deal

with this moment. Why would Dr. Llewellyn take it apart?

She quickly surveyed the scene for missing elements, and suddenly it was clear. The jeweled parts were gone. They were small, crafted to prevent friction between moving parts, but certainly held their own intrinsic value. Her stomach cramped as she mentally calculated the work ahead…and the cost.

Then there was the issue of finding a watchmaker skilled enough to help her. Mr. Gerrit had been one-of-kind. Not just an artisan, but a man willing to listen to her ideas about how to make a clock seaworthy. Only, he'd returned to Holland to take care of his parents.

She clenched her fists and released them with a determined breath. Rather than speculate if there was another man willing to work with a female inventor of no means, she must deal with what she had. Llewellyn's mess.

She tried to put herself in his shoes. He must have taken notes. Did he hope to discover some great secret? She opened drawers around the workspace and quickly found them—drawings and diagrams he'd made while ruthlessly dissecting her small machine and methodically laying out the remains.

With great reluctance, she folded the velvet into the shape of a pouch, the parts of her timepiece gathered roughly inside. She ripped a length of material from her underskirt, cinched the velvet closed, then shoved it into her father's old leather bag along with the diagrams. She tightened her belt over the strap so it was snug against her body, then pulled on her cloak, and lifted the hood over her head.

Avery picked up her basket and exited. Triumph was nearly hers.

*Nearly.*

Back in the hall she re-locked the door as two men

rounded the corner. She jumped guiltily, then did her best to feign nonchalance. After all, they had no reason to suspect her of anything. To them, she would appear a lone widow bringing a basket of food to the good doctor.

She counted the steps that would take her past them. Ten, nine…

They stared at her.

Seven, six…

She risked a covert glance while pretending to fuss with her basket. Something wasn't quite right. One wore the boots of a stableman, the other the neat and frugal garb of shopkeeper. Definitely not patients, not hospital workers. Visitors?

*Don't panic.*

"Good eve, gentlemen." She imitated the accent of barkers down at the wharf. "Just a'leaving some biscuits an' Christmas goodies for the doctor."

Five more steps to the corner. She made the turn while checking on them. They stopped in front of the doctor's door and knocked.

Then suddenly one of the men turned back. "Hey, I know you!"

Avery thought it was quite likely they did if they were the ones who'd robbed her, but she didn't intend to wait and find out.

She sprinted for freedom.

Shouts echoed through the chambers as the men chased after her. Avery rushed and spun down the stairs, before doing a quick reverse. Dr. Llewellyn, from whom she had just liberated her timepiece, stood at the bottom. Fortunately, she had two emergency exit plans.

Avery turned and bounded up the stairs to the next floor, running down a familiar ward where men in recovery were housed until they could either return to their homes or go back to their commissions. Her friend Ned was currently housed here, so she visited regularly and had made many friends.

They were her reinforcements.

A villain tugged the back of her cloak.

And she needed them now!

Avery tossed the checkered cloth from the basket, grabbed the rope hidden inside, then whirled around, swinging the metal-weighted basket at the flunky intent on stopping her.

The contact to his head sent him stumbling backward and into his friend who had followed him blindly into the large room. The walls near the ward's entrance had shelves of fresh linen. She whipped a sheet loose and threw it over the men, gaining precious seconds more.

Back on track she faced her exit. The window at the end of the room never seemed so far away.

"Ned! Plan B! Hurry!"

Ned had a visitor. She hoped that fact would not distract him from her mission. She needed the window open.

Avery ran at full speed, every sense on fire, alive and alert. Ned, a sailor and longtime friend of her family, hobbled on his crutches to the window, worry on his face. He clearly had not taken her plan seriously. Robby, an older mate situated in the middle of the ward, moved faster.

"Mates! Your pans!" he shouted.

Rob's command produced a sea of bedpans, and Avery glanced back to see them hurling through the air from all sides toward the men following her. Avery grinned, certain she would triumph with loyal sailors watching her back. She slid to a stop, breathless, and tossed her cloak out the window before securing the latch at the end of the rope to the one she had installed in the room earlier that day. Scooping her skirts to the side, she slid on her bottom across the windowsill. A shock of cold air hit, freezing her backside as she began to slide out, stalling her momentarily. She glanced back to check the progress of her pursuers.

And in that moment, everything changed.

*She saw him.*

Black hair tied back, blue eyes unwavering, bemused smile teasing his lips.

Avery froze. Time stood still. It was possible after all. Everyone froze. Even the bloody, irritating, thieving villains seemed immobile, wondering what transpired.

Avery inhaled sharply.

Luc was here.

He was the guest visiting Ned.

Ned caught her questioning gaze, before looking away guiltily. Luc had been in town, and Ned had not told her. As usual, Luc had not come to see her. It was only an accident that they were here at this moment in time, that their eyes met in this split second. Perhaps he did not even recognize her.

She would prefer he didn't recognize her. He would know the truth. How could he not? The pain in her chest felt so acute, she thought it must be visible to all.

Four years since he left. Four years he had ignored her. Four years without a word or letter. And yet, in one moment, one awful moment in time, despite everything she'd done—nothing had changed.

She still loved him.

And that love meant one thing—she must jump out the window.

Now.

So she did.

Luc had no time to stop her and no time to see whether she landed safely. He spun from the window to crush a man's face with his fist, silencing him on the tile floor. The other man stopped, decided the odds were against him even if there were no more bedpans to hurl, and slowly backed out, dragging his stunned friend with him.

"Yer making a big mistake, matey!"

Luc took a menacing step forward, towering over the men. "I doubt it—matey."

Harassing shouts from the beds enforced his threat, followed by cheers as Avery's pursuers stumbled hurriedly to vacate.

Luc leaned out the window. A lone figure disappeared into the darkness. She would cut across the park. Familiar territory would make her feel safe.

He unhooked the latch and began to curl the length of rope, a shiver running down his spine at the thought of how easily Avery could have slipped. What the hell was she up to?

Ned and the other men watched and waited. After a long moment, Ned spoke. "That was Avery."

Luc turned on him, a little angry and a little worried. "You think I don't know it?" How could he not know his best friend—the girl who challenged him, the woman who haunted him. He knew her better than he knew himself. That had been the problem. And he had seen firsthand now, how his behavior had affected her. It didn't make him any happier about his choices.

He felt an ache in his chest at the look on her face. It had been relief, followed by dismay and hurt. Not what he'd hoped for, but what could he expect?

"I have to go after her." He swung his cloak around his shoulders.

Ned agreed and climbed back into the bed, careful of his

leg. "Will you tell her I didn't know you were in town until tonight. I hate that she feels betrayed by me. It's bad enough that you abandoned her."

"I didn't—" Luc couldn't defend himself. "It's not like that."

"She doesn't know that." Ned studied him, making Luc just a little uncomfortable. "And truthfully, I'm not sure I understand it either."

Luc sighed. He couldn't explain it. And there wasn't time. He was anxious to find Avery and confirm her safety. "I'll stop by tomorrow."

Ned closed his eyes, a taunting smile on his lips. "She's managed well enough without you. I wouldn't worry."

That sounded even grimmer. He retrieved the innocent-looking basket, surprised by its weight, and fit the rope and accessories back inside. His betrothed was being chased by unsavory characters, her only defense a picnic basket. Nothing to worry about.

Right.

# CHAPTER TWO

She was being followed. Perfect! What next?

Avery pulled off her leather gloves, thankful for their protection sliding down the rope, but after the excitement, her heart still pounded and her hands sweated from exertion. She pushed her cloak over a shoulder to cool down, ducking off the trail and behind a tree to let the man continue past.

She faced Flamsteed House and the Observatory. It was not yet suppertime for the Halleys. She'd visit with them for a bit. Best to wait out her hunters.

She counted. Seventeen steps before he took the downward turn in the path. Only…it was oddly silent.

Careful not to disturb the snow hanging from the tree protecting her, Avery turned her head. The man stood on the path unmoving, his silhouette tall, strong…and familiar.

She sighed, closing her eyes and praying he would leave her. *Please, Luc, just go away*!

"I can hear you thinking."

Damn. And how dare he repeat lines from their past! As if they were still friends, or he really could still hear her thinking!

"Don't be mad. It's a gift."

She heard the smile in his voice. Bastard.

"I just wanted to see you safely home, Avery. Come out from behind the tree. The snow is going to go right through your clothes, and you'll be sniffling on Christmas."

"I have a pistol and I'm happy to make use of it," she said.

"No need, now that I'm her to protect you."

"I meant that I would use it on you."

"Oh. I see." Pause. "That's not much of a holiday welcome for a poor sailor home from sea."

"What makes you worthy of my hospitality?"

He seemed thoughtful. "You're right. I shall have to lean on the holiday sentiment of goodwill to all men."

"Hmph." Avery gave up, but didn't join him. She trudged upward through the snow, toward the observatory. "We are long past you caring for my hospitality, and I need neither your concern nor your protection, Lieutenant."

He followed her off the path, his boots high enough to protect him from the occasional deep banks of snow.

"You have it anyway." He caught up with her. "I don't suppose you want to tell me why two unsavory ruffians were chasing you in a hospital ward."

"I don't suppose," she agreed.

"Right." His leg sunk to his knee in a spot, causing snow to slide into his boot. He kicked through the barrier. "Well, clever escape. I'd rather you use the door next time, but I can't fault your planning."

"Did I seek your approval?" She stopped where she was, pretending to think a moment. "Oh. No, indeed, I did not." She trudged upward, finally reaching the next pathway. Avery knew his tactics. He hoped to flatter her and soften her resolve to ignore him. For some reason, he now wanted to acknowledge her existence.

"How do you like the new Astronomer Royal?" he asked. "I've heard mixed assessments."

Avery liked Halley and felt compelled to defend her new champion. "Professor Halley is brilliant. A bit of a reformed scoundrel, no doubt, but more forward thinking than Flamsteed, whom I respected very much. I don't know if you heard, but Flamsteed's widow took much of his equipment with him, so Professor Halley has a job of it securing the right and proper instruments to further his work." Avery sighed at the setback. "It's a bit frustrating, actually."

She hadn't meant to say so much. Recovering, she continued in silence.

"I can't wait to meet him."

"You needn't follow me. I'm perfectly safe."

"No doubt. But I will see you home regardless."

"I don't want you to 'see me home,' Luc. I want you to go away! It's what you do best, so please don't stop on my account."

He sucked in air. "Point taken."

She regretted the remark, only because it revealed how hurt she'd been. Anxious to leave him behind, Avery hurried to her destination.

Arriving, she pulled the cap off her head, released the braid, and fluffed her flattened hair to appear slightly more presentable. Light illuminated them as the door opened. Professor Halley stood in the glow, smiling.

"I thought that was you, Miss Hilfington! Welcome. And who's your young man?"

Avery bowed politely before introducing Luc. "Sir Lucien Rees, Lieutenant in the Royal Navy." She handed her gloves and cloak to Georges, his butler and everything man. "And he's not my young man. He's been stalking me here."

"Eager for an introduction," Luc added.

"Ah," Halley observed them quietly. "You're a friend to science then?"

"Indeed, sir. Miss Hilfington and I spent our youth at the feet of Flamsteed, and none know these grounds below us or the stars above us, better than Avery and I do."

"Hmm. Old friends? Strange she never mentioned you." He turned to Avery. "You never mentioned him, did you my dear?" He shook his head. "I'm certain I'd remember. Strange, don't you think Lieutenant Rees?"

"Yes, very strange," Luc said, observing Avery for the first time in the light. He swallowed carefully, lest he give himself away. Though she wore all black, the dress fit snugly, showing her form—one that was familiar yet changed.

Changed for the better.

She had always been slender and healthy, but now she seemed to bear her womanly curves with confidence and ease.

As if sensing his regard, she turned on him. Mysterious, dark eyes drew him in while the face of his childhood passed before him. He absorbed her now. The soft, youthful roundness on her cheeks had been replaced with elegant angles. Nothing seemed left of her easy smile except for full plum-colored lips. The hair she'd freed hung past her shoulders in thick waves of rich chocolate, accentuating glowing skin, pink at the cheeks from her latest adventure.

She should have been surrounded by poets instead of scientists. He couldn't imagine any man meeting her and being able leave her. She possessed a lure too strong for a mere mortal to resist, but it was deeper than superficial beauty. Her humor and intelligence engaged, and her heart was kind enough to warm the coldest souls.

Except when she tried to freeze him out. *Hmph. That was new.*

It made the need in his gut even stronger.

He wanted her.

*Now.*

The sound of Professor Halley clearing his throat brought Luc back to the moment. The doorman reached for his basket, and Luc handed him the 'goodies'. "You must try these. Miss Hilfington's exclusive recipe. One taste is an adventure," he explained.

Avery whisked the basket from the men. "Alas, nothing but crumbs remain. They were for our recovering sailors, and considering the food at the hospital, anything I make is delicious by comparison." She set the basket by the floor near her cloak, scowling when Luc winked at her.

"I've come to you with a different issue, Professor," Avery said, her hand protecting the leather bag across her shoulders.

"Indeed," Halley said.

"Indeed?" Luc repeated, curious.

"Indeed," Avery answered.

"Let us away to the Octagon Room. I've a table set up we can use. Georges," Halley called to the doorman. "Fetch us some tea, good man."

Luc followed Avery and Halley through the modest rooms of what the town referred to as Flamsteed House, named after the first Astronomer Royal who had been responsible for the structure. It had been years since Luc had been in the Octagon Room, but the high windows and pleasing shape did not disappoint. The safety of darkness encased the room except for a candelabrum opposite the large telescope Halley had set up. Halley handed him a house torch and the two proceeded to light the candles around the edge of the room, illuminating it.

"I saw you from here earlier." Halley put the torches away. "The trees moved unnaturally, as if from deer or human, but the purposeful direction led me to believe it human."

"You've keen observation, sir," Luc said, thinking it would be quite difficult to see in the darkness unless it was one's daily habit—but then for Halley, it was.

"Observation is the most important skill for a scientist of the natural world. This room is perfect for social stargazing. Alas, for the real work, we must retreat to the shed in the back. A poorly designed observatory this has turned out to be." He winked engagingly. "But I shall fix that—with luck, persuasion, and a small bit from the king's purse."

Luc had heard of Halley's adventures, but found his company very easy on acquaintance, and he seemed genuinely fond of Avery—who apparently trusted him more than Luc. She opened the leather bag and revealed a velvet cloth fastened with a bit of skirt if he wasn't mistaken. He studied Avery again, wondering what circumstance warranted such quick and drastic measures.

"What's this, my dear?" Halley asked.

Avery's voice was husky. She opened the cloth revealing beautifully cut elements of a mechanical instrument. "It *was* my sea watch."

Halley gasped at the array of parts. "Good God, my girl! Who did this?"

Georges entered with the tray of tea.

"There's been a catastrophe, Georges! An abomination to science and technology!" His fist landed firmly on the table. "We're going to need something stronger than tea!"

Georges hurried out and back with a bottle of amber liquid apparently stored not too far away. Luc decided then and there that Halley was the best astronomer Greenwich had ever seen.

"Don't worry," he assured Avery. "My wife is in London with friends 'til the eve before Christmas. Drink up!" Halley raised his glass. "To the stars."

"The stars," they repeated before taking a drink.

Avery sighed. She looked weary.

"That helps. Thank you, Professor Halley. It's been a difficult week."

"Well, at least you found it, and you found the villain."

"Villains, it seems." She looked at the timepiece. "It will take weeks to put this right. I'm not sure who is available to even help."

"Gerrit has left already, then?" Halley asked.

Avery nodded.

"Damn his good heart."

Avery smiled.

"Who is Gerrit?" Luc interrupted.

"A watchmaker from London," Avery explained. "He crafted and helped assemble the parts from my design." She stared forlornly at the parts. "He was brilliant."

"Professor," Avery's eyes implored. "I can't bring it home. That's where it was stolen."

"You can leave it here until needed," Halley said.

"Thank you, sir."

"What was so special about it," Luc asked.

"It was a sea watch. With latitude and Greenwich time you could calculate longitude at sea."

Luc straightened, astonished, the pieces of the puzzle falling into place. "You're a longitude lunatic?"

She stiffened, defensive. "I am not. I have a legitimate solution."

"You and every other loon in Greenwich."

She tossed her hair, and lifted her chin, dark eyes blazing with passion.

"Perhaps," Luc adjusted to her defensive stance, "wrong thing to say."

Halley patted his shoulder. "Let me pour you some more. This is getting interesting."

"What I do is none of your business, Lieutenant," Avery declared.

"On the contrary, my dear, as your fiancé, it is very much my business."

She gasped loudly, her mouth remaining open in shock until Professor Halley helped by lifting her glass for her to take a sip.

"Indeed," Halley said. "Very interesting."

Avery took the brandy and threw back the contents in one gulp before clunking the glass on the table.

"You, Lieutenant," she spoke with precision, "are most certainly *not* my fiancé."

"Really? Because according to the agreement of our parents, our betrothal has been longstanding, my dear."

"I released you from that commitment." Avery frowned, confused. "Before you left four years ago."

"It hasn't been four years."

"Yes, four years!"

Luc resisted smiling, knowing he provoked her further by contradicting. "Three years, eleven months and five days."

Avery's eyes filled with pain. Luc immediately regretted dredging up the memory. He'd left without saying goodbye after being a constant companion most of their lives. By her interpretation it had been callous. For him, survival.

"I sent you a letter, freeing you from our parents' commitment. You are not betrothed to me." Her voice became huskier. "You have no relationship, or right to claim responsibility for me. And any childhood association we may have had is long passed."

"May have had? Avery, we didn't sneeze without the other one nearby to say 'God bless you.' Of course our parents had reason to think their agreement would be good news to us."

"I must confess, I do observe a very magnetic connection between you," Halley inserted.

"Our connection is gone—magnetic, childhood, or otherwise. You made it very clear you wanted it that way." Avery's voice caught, before she cleared her throat. "I have no idea why you now insist on resurrecting the past. I released you."

"I never received a letter."

"Well," Halley said, "that could mean you are still betrothed, and without a chaperone attending you, the circumstances are becoming increasingly in favor of it."

Avery stared at Luc, shaking her head. A new thought seemed to pain her even further.

"Then, if I understand correctly, believing you were in fact my betrothed, you deliberately avoided me on every visit you made to Greenwich in the last three years, eleven months and five days."

Halley sucked air through pursed lips. "Bad form, young man."

"Well, it's not as if I was willingly betrothed."

"And not improving your position, Lieutenant," he noted.

"I was not willingly betrothed either," Avery said. "And since my letter seems to have been lost, let me clarify for you right now."

Luc couldn't help but admire how beautiful she was when inflamed with righteous fury. Her flashing eyes glittered from reflected candlelight, while her body tensed, drawing his attention to her modest décolletage and destining him to the lowest form of man in her eyes. This was the consequence of staying away from her too long. The mere hint of ivory skin overwhelmed his usual restraint. She waited until his eyes lifted. He saw her surprise at his slow survey before hostility took over.

"I release you from any and all legitimate commitment to me, either real or inferred. You may continue on you way. You have no further obligation, Lieutenant Rees."

Avery turned with control to Halley. "Thank you, Professor, for the refreshment and for allowing me to leave what remains of my timepiece here until I can gather my thoughts and resources."

"Of course, my dear."

She turned and charged out. Luc followed, their farewells abrupt at best. Regardless of how she felt, he would not let her walk home alone. The villains might still be about, or she could fall on ice and be injured. Or worse, she would have time alone to remind herself why he was so hateful.

Outside, she walked silently in the night until they were well away from the observatory. Once protected by the darkness and sound proofing of snow-laden trees, she turned on him.

"You may leave me!"

"It's not safe."

"This is Greenwich, not London. Please. Leave me alone."

Luc wished it were that easy. He could not see into her eyes but knew from the reflection of her white skin that she faced him. He wanted to reach out and pull her to him, keep her warm from the decreasing temperatures. He wanted to do other things to warm her but he had lost that right, along with any affection that might have permitted it.

If he had only heard wrath in her tone, he might have obeyed and followed at a safe distance. He might have believed there was no hope for him.

But he knew her.

He heard the catch in her throat. He recognized the anger attempting to hide the pain he had caused. It gave him hope where there had been only false confidence a short while ago. And hope made him stubborn. "I cannot."

She gave a feminine growl of frustration. "Then you leave me no choice."

Luc waited for her to explain. Instead, he caught the shadow of a dark object swinging toward him and realized her lethal basket was about to make contact.

# CHAPTER THREE

He ducked.

Of course he would, the bastard. Unfortunately, the power of her swing threw Avery the slightest degree off balance. In dry weather, it would not have been an issue. On the icy path, conditions were substantially less favorable.

She wobbled. Her feet stumbled for balance. Suddenly he was there, grasping her waist to support her, then losing his own balance. Good lord, he was going to take her down with him!

Somehow, being a man of quick wits and limber parts, he was able to twist around as they fell, protecting her head from the hard path. Instead, she landed atop him, her breasts on his nose, her face in the snow.

"Ah!" Cold ice met her mouth and she shut it instantly, reaching her hands out to push up. Only her hands sank, deep into the piled snow, trapping her further.

"Well, this is an interesting turn of events." The vibration of his speech tickled her, infuriating her further.

"Don't talk." Her voice was muffled in the ice.

"What?"

There was that tickle again. She squeaked unwillingly, and tried again to climb out.

"Stop wiggling, Avery. You're making it worse."

She couldn't control the wiggle! He reached for her ribs. Oh no. Not her ribs. She squealed. "Stop!"

"I'm just going to lift you—" He lifted enough to slide her elbows out and lower her bosom from his face. To be fair, suffocating that way wasn't entirely his fault. Unfortunately, his thumbs went too far into her ribs.

"No!" Her body convulsed wildly in reaction. "Stop," she laughed. "It tickles."

His chest heaved in humor beneath her. "Nice to know some things haven't changed." His thumbs gave a deliberate poke.

She opened her palm on his face and smashed a handful of hard snow on him.

"Hey!"

His complaint gave her an opening to push more snow into his mouth. "That should do the trick."

He spit it out at her.

"Careful." She ducked.

"That was unfair snowfare if ever I saw it."

She placed a hand on his chest to leverage into a seated position. "You were tickling me."

"Not intentionally."

"That last time it was." He squeezed her knee through woolen skirts. She bucked in reaction then slapped his hand, furious at this laughter. "It's not funny. Let me up."

"I'm the one buried, in case you haven't noticed, though quite happy." He squeezed again obtaining a similar reaction. "A little to the left next ti—"

Avery pushed a pile of snow over his face. He would be duly frozen and rightly so. Though considering his disgraceful thoughts, perhaps lower would be more effective.

"Bloody hell, that's cold. And it's down my collar."

"You've grown depraved, Luc. You disappoint me, most assuredly."

He grunted. "And you've lost your sense of humor, old friend. Most assuredly."

"I have not." Just to prove it she pushed another pile of snow on his face from the other side. He roared underneath the ice, but was muffled by her second shove. Her eyes had adjusted to darkness and Luc was now headless. "There, you see." She gave a genuine smile for the first time in his company. "Most amusing."

He desperately shoveled the snow from his face while she pushed off him, inadvertently pressing below his hips. He gasped at the sudden weight.

"Sorry." She fell backward on her bottom, sliding the necessary inches down the slight incline and onto the path.

"I'm all right."

"Too bad." She stood and removed her leather gloves to empty out the frozen crystals while watching Luc wriggle and struggle in the deep snow. "Do you need a hand?"

"Yes."

"I'll send help. Goodnight."

"Avery Hilfington!"

"Don't shout. Honestly, Luc," she taunted. "Where's your sense of humor?"

"It froze and fell off with the rest of my assets, love." He held up a hand. "Now help me out. Carefully. I don't want you to crack your head after all my efforts."

Avery planted her boots and reached out a hand. His enclosed it—large and warm through his glove, despite the cold. She pulled him up, and he wrapped an arm around her, pulling her to his chest. The man seemed to generate heat. She was tempted to lean in and accept the warmth.

Instead she stepped away. Or at least tried.

"One moment." He wrapped his other arm around her until she was pressed snugly against him. "I need to get warm."

Avery's stomach clenched, her body immobile, waiting. Finally he released her.

She retrieved her basket, fuming. "Don't ever take liberties with me again, Lieutenant. Nor pretend that nearly four years of your disregard have not taken a toll. They have."

Avery turned back to the path, surprised by the hot tears warming her cheeks. She wiped them instantly, moving quick and nimble across the snowy path.

"I'm sorry."

The softly spoken words slipped into a hopeful crack in her heart before she sealed it, silently continuing on her way, her weakness only irritating her further.

He caught up with her. "I know I lost all rights as your friend when I left without saying goodbye."

"And never saying hello when you came back."

"I didn't know you realized."

Her throat tightened dangerously, and she had to swallow in order to speak. "You did not think in our small town, where you and I grew up and are known virtually by all—you did not think someone would ask me about your visit, or say, 'Nice to see young Rees looking so well, eh, Miss Hilfington? The sea surely agrees with him.' Or, 'How about Rees fighting off pirates in New Providence.' Or the baker, reminding me how *our* Rees 'kept the Spanish fleet on the run.' You even have Ned lying for you now."

"I only arrived today. Ned didn't know I was coming to visit."

"No doubt you would have sworn him to secrecy."

"I didn't want you to be hurt."

"How do you think it felt to be the one person left uninformed, especially when I was the one who cared the most…save your mother."

"Humiliating, no doubt."

She stopped in her tracks. He sounded contrite. Was that regret in his voice? She sighed, an old hurt burning her heart. Did any of it matter anymore? "If humiliation was the only affect of your abandonment, it would have been easily borne, but you belittle the friendship we once had and make light of the years we shared if you think humiliation was anything but the least of my feelings."

She continued on her way, reaching the street. Lights from some of the park-facing homes made her path clearer while a cold breeze whisked through her damp clothes making even her bones feel brittle.

"Avery," he said.

Five more houses and she would be home. A welcome fire and hot bath would do the trick.

"Avery," he called again.

"What?" Avery waited. Indeed, there was nothing she would like better than an explanation that would take the pain away. "What, Luc? What can you say? Were you afraid that as your fiancé I would insist you marry me? That is a horror. I suppose one cannot be blamed to fear an unwelcome marriage."

"It wasn't—"

She paused. Waited. Felt a glimmer of hope. "It wasn't what?"

Nothing. Then finally…

"It wasn't what you think."

"Will you tell me then, what in fact it was?"

Silence.

"I cannot."

Avery nodded. Her blood burned to her toes suddenly

warming her. His explanation proved his continued disregard. Only a fool would believe otherwise. The last glimmer of hope faded out.

"I see. Well, I don't expect you will be in town very long. I wish you very merry. Goodnight and goodbye."

With that, Avery turned her back on the man who had finally and truly broken her heart.

Luc moved slowly. He wanted to follow and explain. Instead he turned and walked the short distance to his family's manor. It had been difficult avoiding her the few times he had been home. He'd been a fool to think he'd been successful in hiding it from her. He'd made every effort not to catch even a glimpse of her. Once he had seen her across the park. It had been mid-September the year before. The sun still shone warmly and she'd worn a vibrant blue dress, her hair tied loosely behind her catching the breeze as she strode confidently.

He'd wanted to follow her. See her. Hold her once again. The possibility had made him hungrier than ever.

It had taken an act of will to pack his bag and leave immediately. Leaving her four years ago was still the hardest thing he'd ever done. He knew he couldn't do it twice. That's why he made sure he never saw her. He wasn't ready yet. And until that time, he had to resist giving into the power she held over him. For it was a power. His body still tingled from her nearness. He breathed wintry air welcoming even icy pain to alleviate the sensations that ran through him from when she'd been near.

He removed his gloves and accepted the frozen sting in his fingers as a well-deserved punishment for what he had done. He had abandoned her. There was no denying it.

And until he could win her back, no explanation for his behavior would make sense.

# CHAPTER FOUR

Avery spread her favorite blueberry preserves over a scone, surprised at how hungry she was this morning. But of course, yesterday had been very busy, and she had gone to her room early without supper. She'd been too upset from seeing Luc to even tolerate the smell of food, and it had been a long restless night after that.

She'd snuck out for an early morning walk and the sunny, cold freshness reinvigorated her. By breakfast she felt less preoccupied by Luc, so perhaps confrontation was the road to recovery. Yes, excellent. That must be it. Yesterday was a shock, but now that she'd absorbed it, life was normal again.

"Good morning, my dear. It's beautiful today, is it not?" Her mother whisked into the room bringing the scent of lavender perfume with her. Cheerily, she opened a window and breathed in frosty air. "Ah! Wonderful." An icy breeze shot inside and ruffled the tablecloth. "Oh, it's freezing!" Her mother slammed the window shut. "Enough of that." She took a seat across from Avery. "You look better. How are the blueberries?"

Her mother had gone overboard with a holiday breakfast

and was decidedly chipper.

Avery nodded, her mouth full, indicating her approval. Her mother smiled, satisfied.

Avery viewed the array of food, and slathered one last portion of preserves on the scone. Far too much for two people, but all her favorites. When was the last time her mother had requested scones *and* raisin biscuits. A calculation started innocently in her head as she looked at the smoked ham and scrambled eggs with spinach.

Then it clicked.

September, the year before.

Her stomach lurched. Then February prior. Not on her birthday, that would have made sense. In November the year before. She started to work backward, oblivious to the dark blueberries dripping off her fork. Finally she swallowed hard, stunned at the realization.

Without warning, Avery felt her eyes burn in betrayal.

"Avery? What is it?"

She slowly put down her fork, appetite gone. "You knew."

Her mother waited, eyes wide, for an explanation. Only now she looked guilty.

"You knew Luc was in town, and you've known every time. You make my favorites when he is in town."

"Nonsense. I request your favorites because I love you." She poured tea avoiding Avery's eyes. "If Luc was in town, perhaps it merely reminded me how much I love you and how grateful I am you are not yet married."

"What happened to my letter?"

The teapot froze midair. Finally her mother put it down, releasing a heavy sigh. "You've seen him, I presume."

"Last night. Visiting Ned." Her mother didn't need to know the details.

"And you went alone. It was dark when you returned.

You know I don't like that. It's not proper or safe."

"It's Greenwich. Everyone knows me, Mother. Most everyone at least."

"The town has grown since your childhood. Don't over estimate the kindness of strangers. Especially men."

"Especially not men, Mother. But you've very nicely avoided my question."

"Yes, I have, haven't I?" She sipped her tea, unaffected. "Have you decided on a gown for the ball?"

"Mother!"

"Oh, you're no fun anymore."

Avery couldn't help feeling hurt by that. Especially since Luc had said very nearly the same thing. But they didn't understand how she felt. She'd been abandoned by her friend and betrayed by those closest to her. The shock of it was hard to absorb.

"Perhaps it's easier being the one doing the betraying."

Her mother stiffened. "I was protecting you."

"From what? The truth? From having the least bit of say in my own life?"

"It's nothing like that."

"What happened to the letter?" Avery could hardly bear to imagine it. Did her mother read it?

"You were only seventeen. Too young to think rationally."

"I've been thinking rationally since I was born." Avery nearly shouted the words.

"Oh, yes." Her mother teased. "That's the problem."

Before Avery could control her frustration, a tear tumbled down her cheek. She stood up to leave, frustrated and angry at being manipulated, and irritated by tears that continued to plague her. "I am not the one who is flawed."

Her mother had the grace to look remorseful. Avery knew she did not intend to be cruel, but she hated the lies, she hated that others had conspired against her, and she hated having no one to turn to.

"Don't leave." Her mother implored. "There's still mini-pies on the way."

Avery tried again. "What happened to the letter?"

"I took it before it could be received."

"And?"

"And I read it. I thought the two of you would be back together in no time. I certainly didn't think Luc would be gone so long. Goodness knows the torture you both suffered when he was away for school. It was obvious to all of us, his parents included, that you were both of an age when things were changing, and an early marriage might not be a bad thing. That's all."

"Where is my letter now?"

Her mother scooped some butter onto her plate along with a portion of ham. "Ashes, dear. Sorry."

Avery nodded. Surprisingly calm. The most gut-wrenching missive she'd ever had to craft had been burned by her mother. "I have errands. Excuse me."

Her mother stood and met her at the doorway, unshed tears indicating her regret over their argument.

"Avery, I'm sorry about the past. It's just that I could not bear for you to suffer more. I never thought Luc would stay away. Why, he did not even visit *me*!" Avery smiled at her mother's attempt at affronted vanity. "I told the servants not to mention his name or alert you that he was home for I knew it would cause you pain. I only took your letter because…what you and Luc have is something few people ever find. I thought for certain you would have found your way by now."

Avery nodded again, accepting the apology, though still stinging from the betrayal.

"We did find our way, Mother. I officially broke off our

betrothal last night. It is now very clear to both parties that our lives are set on different courses. Now we are each free to follow them."

"Well." Her mother stood frozen, absorbing the news. Finally she blinked. "That's dismal Christmas news."

Avery laughed, wiping the evidence of emotion from her cheeks. "It was an ending long overdue. The new year will bring a new chapter. All will be well."

"Any news on your timepiece?"

Avery hesitated at the door. "None as yet, but I have a lead to follow up."

"Is that one of your errands? Can't the magistrate handle this?" Her mother sounded worried.

"They have already completed their investigation and made it perfectly clear an invention made by a woman cannot be worth much, let alone their valuable resources."

Her mother frowned. "I know Mary is going with you, but take Campbell as well. Best not to be alone, and Campbell could effectively clobber anyone should the need arise."

"I've no intention of clobbering anyone…" She recalled last night and added, "…today. But I'll bring them with me."

Her mother agreed, but continued to block her way. A delicate hand clasped hers. "And you forgive me?"

"Mother." Avery huffed, still upset.

"I didn't raise you to be unforgiving." At Avery's silent scowl, her mother quickly added. "Or cruel to the elderly."

Avery laughed out loud. At just forty-one, her mother was still very vibrant and beautiful.

"Since you are bordering on ancient, I will forgive you," Avery said. "But, Mother, what you did was wrong and unfair to me and Luc. Please don't ever interfere like that again."

Her mother's eyes widened. "But I'm your mother! That's impossible!"

"Mother!" Avery shook her had exasperated.

"Hurry along. You can keep your forgiveness until I'm on my deathbed." She went back to the table, unrepentant, and reached for a scone, talking to herself. "Not interfere? That makes no sense at all."

Avery gave up. If she was to have any control over her life, she would simply need to keep her plans to herself. She clutched the watch hanging over her breast. That meant she would be investigating on her own.

"You've a knack for investing, son. Your mother is in good hands."

"Thank you, Uncle Harry." Luc glanced up from the papers, with a contented smile.

"And your wool supply has increased twenty percent in the last three years. Seems like your gamble paid off."

"Science, Uncle Harry. By crossbreeding we've raised sheep that are heartier and producing longer and finer wool. Though I had not planned on purchasing the adjacent property." Luc had been conservative with their funds but the extra property was too good to pass. "Thankfully it's been a boon."

He and his father had often spent time in this room, discussing the challenges of funding a small baronetcy. He wished his father could see the fruits of their labors for many calculations had manifested favorably. Luc had harvested their land early this year despite advice otherwise. It had been his first firm decision about the land since inheriting the baronetcy. The steward had always managed without him.

Luc now hoped his studies during the dull hours at sea would prove beneficial. He had some thoughts about farming and breeding sheep that made use of his knack for science and astronomy. It gave him options, and they were options he'd earned and created for himself. There was immense satisfaction and confidence in that.

"I heard you've been courted by the Naval Office. Any chance you'll be returning to sea?"

Luc was not surprised by the question. His uncle was still very well tied into the workings at the Office. "I've not had time to give it my full consideration," he said honestly.

"Master and Commander doesn't tempt you?"

He grinned. "It does." His skills at navigation were largely due to Avery's obsession with the stars, and they had not gone unnoticed. "As does the thought of working closer to home. And London has its comforts."

"The Office pays well enough, even on land."

"But the paperwork."

"There is that," his uncle agreed. "The Office, the land, or the sea…which is it to be, for my nephew Luc must choose from three."

"You shall have to wait and see," Luc chimed. The command would take him far away. The Naval Office in London, just a riverboat ride from Greenwich. Or, he could become entirely self-sufficient and build the small property that had been in his family for years. He wondered how Avery would feel about that?

As if reading his thoughts, his uncle mentioned her. "Miss Hilfington has turned out to be an impressive woman. But then, she was a brilliant child. Full of adventure and determination."

"Yes." Luc didn't know what to add to that. His uncle said nothing by chance. The man was a master of fishing out information. Luc organized the books while his uncle gazed out the window.

"And she strides with such purpose!"

Luc's head snapped up at that. He went to the window, falling for the bait. Harry grinned wickedly. "You missed her. Off to the market with Mary and Campbell. Good odds they'll stop for hot chocolate at the Park Tavern before coming home. Miss Hilfington never denies Mary," he shared, "and of course she will want to make herself scarce to give Mary and Campbell a few moments of privacy. Probably step away to browse the shops."

"I wasn't aware that Miss Hilfington posed a threat to the crown."

"We make it our business to know what's going on in the lives of Britain's great minds. And I do reside at the hospital's pensioner quarters. Not much goes without notice."

Luc nodded, still staring out the window. "We have not really had time to catch up yet. I don't really know what is going on in her life." He only knew the pieces of information his mother and others had shared. No longer Avery's closest confidante nor the object of her affection, he could not claim to know her heart like he once did. Yet, hers had always been steadfast. It seemed impossible she could have changed much in the areas that mattered.

"Luc," his uncle interrupted his thoughts. "Make sure Avery is more careful. I'd hate to see something happen to her."

The very suggestion caused a stabbing pain in his chest and an urgent pulsing in his blood. "She is very capable." And independent and stubborn, he added silently.

"No doubt."

"I have a notion to visit Ned, then get a drink in town, a hot chocolate perhaps."

"Good idea, my boy. Enjoy yourself." His uncle sat back

in a big chair and lifted his feet to the window. "Mayhap I'll see you later."

"Don't worry, Uncle. I'll not let anything happen to her."

Luc was already out the door, the choices that would determined the path of his life forgotten. There was one key piece to it all, and he had to make sure she remained safe.

"Three peppermint sticks and two chocolates, please." Avery paid for the treats before turning to Campbell.

"You're not joining us, Miss Hilfington?" he asked.

"If you don't mind, I thought I'd just run next door and see if there are any new science volumes," Avery said. "I'll not be long."

Campbell nodded, "I don't mind the time to catch up with Mary. Thank you, Miss Hilfington."

Avery smiled and stopped by the table where Mary waited, and asked her to look after her packages. She chewed on a piece of peppermint and slipped out the door, breathing the fresh, cold air with relief. There was no time for the bookstore. Checking her watch, Avery estimated it was six minutes at a brisk pace to reach the stable yard, and six minutes return—if her luck held. That gave her three minutes to make inquiries.

She moved quickly, head down against the light wind. When she reached the yards, very few were about. Lunching no doubt. She found the man in charge and asked him some questions, but he was decidedly unhelpful.

"Sorry, miss. You've described the attire of about every man who works 'ere."

"He was about medium build with brown hair." Avery

waited hopefully. Nothing. "Very well. Thank you."

It had been a long shot, she supposed. She exited from the side and found herself on a tiny street, the backside of the Cock 'n Bull Tavern. It was one of the more male-oriented establishments, and Avery had never had cause to visit it. She noticed with surprise that the there was a small watchmakers sign in the shop next to it. The shop was little more than a small room with a window, but there was someone inside, his head down, working away.

She entered, curious.

The man bent over a standing magnifying glass, working intently. He looked up and when their eyes met, Avery recognized him instantly. He was the shopkeeper—her second pursuer. She froze, swallowing hard, before she realized there was nothing in her appearance that should give herself away. She looked entirely different than she did yesterday. Nothing about her said widow. Her red dress was festive. Yet he appeared to have the same reaction that Avery did. For a moment they stared, neither sure who would make the first move.

To her surprise, it was him.

He ran.

There was a back door to his shop, and Avery shoved her foot out in time to stop him from closing and locking it.

"Ouch!" She pulled the knob, but he was already on the move. "Wait! I just want to talk to you!" She ran down the hall after him.

She didn't really know what she would say. Discovering him was a surprise. But it made sense now, the two men. The merchant and the laborer who knew each other because their businesses were so close.

She reached the end of the hall and turned to see him taking a flight of stairs with the vigor of a younger man.

Avery followed, a swinging door at the top nearly knocking her backward. She pushed the door forcefully, spotting her target as he raced down another short hall.

He glanced back. Their eyes met. Then he turned and was gone.

Avery ran after him and wound up in storage space that smelled of ale. A cold keg blocked her way. It *was* ale. She climbed over and entered the public room, pure instinct saving her. She ducked. Just in time. Something crashed loudly against the wall behind her. A heavy pewter stein. Her heart pounded erratically. That could have killed her! Furious, she shouted.

"Stop, you bastard!"

Never in her life had she sworn…at least not out loud.

Well, at least not in public. In a room full of men. In a room full of men who had gone suddenly silent at her appearance.

She realized too late the crowded room was the upstairs quarters of the Cock 'n' Bull. He had led her into the middle of a lair. Dozens of men huddled around tables, smoking and drinking.

Dear lord, Greenwich was too small for this kind of blunder. Perhaps the heavy smoke would prevent anyone from recognizing her.

The watchmaker leapt forward, climbing onto a table and jumping across others until he reached the window. Avery, furious and determined to stop him, followed suit, grateful for her sturdy boots to crunch and stomp the few brazen hands that reached out for her.

"Not now!" Honestly, would not one of them help? "Stop that man!"

They stared at her. Then at him. Then at her. Then chatter started up again as they all decided it was none of their business.

"Excellent." Avery scowled, hurrying across a long communal table at a dangerous speed. Her feet slipped, and she slid over wet, varnished wood, barely maintaining her balance, while the men adeptly lifted their drinks out of her path.

The watchmaker opened the window at the end of the room, and with a quick wicked grin back at her, turned, jumped and disappeared.

Avery regained her balance on the table, grasped her skirts, and jumped from the table to the window. She was vaguely aware of the widening eyes of an ancient-looking man as she hurdled toward him, landed on the floor with force, then slid across the windowsill, ready to leap.

"Avery! Stop!"

Avery turned. Luc stood behind her at the other end of the room, his hair tousled as if he'd been running. He tried to navigate the crowd.

Avery looked back to the street. The villain was escaping. There was no time to waste. This man had stolen her timepiece, and might be part of the ring responsible for stealing other important tools to solve longitude. She couldn't wait. Luc would understand someday, but today she had something she had to do.

She jumped.

# CHAPTER FIVE

"No!" Luc vaulted through the air, his heart pounding. He leapt table to table across the room, oblivious of whose ale he knocked over.

He reached the window, expecting disaster.

Avery remained below. She'd landed like a bullet in a large snow pile, her skirt up to her ears, encased over her head. She didn't move. He prayed she was alive—without two broken legs. Suddenly there was movement. Powder flew about as she appeared to punch her way free, clambering over and out of the shoveled snow until she reached the side of the road, liberated from her landing pad.

"The girl's got gumption," his uncle said. Luc noticed him for the first time at the window, shaking his head at the sight below.

Avery pulled at her dress, adjusting it as she looked around.

"Up High Road!" his uncle shouted, pointing the direction.

Avery took the hint, and after a slight wobble, ran toward Greenwich High.

"What are you doing?" Luc hollered at his uncle.

"Assisting, my good man. What are *you* doing?"

Luc looked down at the road. Avery and the other man had dispersed a great deal of the snow that would have made the jump safe.

"Not that way." His uncle pulled him by the scruff of the neck and redirected to the front entrance. "The stairs. Hurry. She's fast and might actually catch the bugger!"

Luc wasted no time. He was out the door of the tavern in an instant, running full speed and grateful the roads were fairly dry from the morning sun. He caught Avery in no time. She was at a crossroads, looking for a sign.

"That way," she said, breathless. "He's heading back toward the stables."

"How do you know?"

"His buddy works there. I'm certain of it."

Luc grabbed her hand and they raced together, making a circle to the backside of the stable yard. The gate was open when they got there. Luc held Avery back.

"Let me. If he's got a pistol, I'd prefer your red dress not be the target."

She nodded agreeably.

"A telling response, indeed," he grumbled to himself.

The yard was quiet except for the occasional huff of a horse settling. Luc stepped forward cautiously looking left and right as he made his way through the center of the stables.

Avery whispered from behind. "Maybe I was wrong."

He turned around in time to see that she wasn't. A loud neigh sounded before three horses came barreling down on Avery.

"Avery," he reached out his hand beckoning. "Run!"

Avery turned, and stared in momentary shock. Luc ran and yanked her to attention, pulling her along roughly, while desperately checking for any open stall. Avery did the same.

Until the thunder grew louder.

"Luc." Fear strangled from her throat as they continued to run. There was no time left to find a stall. Terror filled her voice. "Luc!"

He was amazed she could scream while running so fast, but the sound of his name, and knowing that she depended on him, seemed to fill him with super human strength.

Taking a chance, he kicked through the wood of the closest stall, wrapped an arm around her waist, and jumped.

The angry stallions continued past until there were only the disturbed whinnies of those left behind. Slowly Luc opened his eyes.

Avery was tucked against his chest, hands up protecting her face. Eventually she lowered them to his chest, peeking about to see if they were safe.

A deep sigh of relief went through him. She was alive, roughed up, but relatively unharmed. He carefully brushed hay off her face, and out of her hair. She laid still, soft puffs of air caressing his chin as her heartbeat fought to settle.

"I don't know what you thought you would do once you caught up with that man."

"I just wanted to talk to him," she said.

"Talk?" he laughed. "Indeed."

"I promised my mother there would be no clobbering today," she confessed wryly.

"I'm relieved. Because there is something I must do."

Avery gazed back into his eyes, curious. She truly did not know. At least not until his free hand cupped her cheek, and his lips grazed her forehead. He closed his eyes and breathed in the past. Despite the earthy smell of the stables, she emanated lemons and apricots. The memories filled him instantly. Chasing her. Her chasing him. Lying in the grass as children, looking at clouds. Lying in the grass when they were older, looking at stars…his hand reaching out to hers.

"I remember you," he said, nuzzling her hair. "I've missed your scent."

"Luc…" Her voice was husky and uncertain, but her body arched into him.

He touched his lips to her shoulder and turned his nose to the side of her neck, inhaling her like a drug, before rubbing upward, like an animal marking his mate. He would mark her. Today, he would mark her as his.

"Luc," she gasped. "We mustn't. We, we…"

Luc looked into her dark, midnight eyes and saw confusion, desire…and his future.

"Yes, Avery." He lowered his mouth to hers, ever so slowly, savoring this unexpected gift. "Yes," he breathed over her lips. Then finally, commanding, determined, with no turning back, "Yes. We must."

And he did what he had been dying to do for three years, eleven months, and six days.

Avery's mind became incapable of reason. Her will abandoned her. It was terrifying. Terrifying…and yet comforting. For she was in Luc's arms, and she knew despite the years and even her own feelings that he would never let anything happen to her. The link from their childhood gave her that right. She saw it in the depths of his eyes, witnessed it in the concern on his face, and felt it in the gentleness of his touch. In one moment, their souls reconnected and instantly her world came back into balance. The darkness lifted, and a memory of them laughing as they ran across the park echoed in her mind, melting her heart in a way nothing else could.

She closed her eyes and exhaled softly into his mouth, their breath mingling as their bodies entwined.

"Yes," she agreed with a welcoming sigh.

His lips touched hers softly, and the warmth combined with delicate moisture against the dry chill of her lips, made her fold into him more deeply, wanting his heat and much, much more.

Mouths glided over each other, leisurely exploring. He had kissed her once, before that fateful day their mothers had revealed the betrothal agreement. It had been a long overdue kiss even then, built upon months of touching, hand-holding, and intense longing to feel ever closer, though perhaps not understanding all that it meant. His kiss had been curious, then exploratory, and both were relieved that the build up had been worth the wait. It had made Avery feel like she had never found her true home until that moment.

This kiss was different.

Exploration turned to conquest. Luc gathered her in then rolled on top of her, letting her feel the weight, strength, and power of him. Then the tongue that seemed to taste and tease, gently invaded, commanding her response. It was a response she gave willingly, as she threaded her hands through thick, soft hair and pulled him more completely into her. She savored every inch of him, wanting to celebrate this reunion of their bodies.

When his lips lifted for air, and traveled down her throat, lingering before sending heat across her shoulder, she nearly shouted the words locked in her heart.

*Nearly.*

She panted for air instead, her heartbeat increasing as the warmth of his large hand came inside her cloak and slid over the front piece of her chest.

"Oh, Luc…" she sighed with unaccountable delight, oblivious to the dangers of desire.

Until another sound alerted her.

A whinny.

Avery's eyes fluttered open, to look directly into Luc's bright blue ones. They stared at each other for a moment, both smiling, pleasantly numb to their circumstances.

"It seems," Luc said quietly, while leaning to whisper in her ear, "that we have interrupted someone's nap."

Avery turned her head trying to ignore the fact that Luc deliberately tickled her ear with his breath.

In the stall, a young foal lay curled in the corner, awakened by the commotion, its head cocked curiously as it stared at them.

"I believe we may have scandalized our youthful friend," she said.

"Umm…" Luc nibbled on the flesh of her ear. "Believe me, love. I haven't yet started to be scandalous."

Avery came to her senses. "We have to leave. Someone will wonder about the horses. And the watchmaker…he might return and catch us unaware." Avery tried to get up, but she was still tangled, and mostly trapped by Luc—a place she enjoyed except for her mounting concern over being discovered. "Luc—"

He sighed, and kissed her on the forehead. "We will talk about this later."

"I'd rather we just do more of this later." Her youthful frankness came back with the sudden comfort she had in his presence. Though he laughed, she instantly regretted revealing so much. If he wanted to talk, it was no doubt to explain this was unintentional. Perhaps he would apologize. He pulled her to her feet and into his arms for another kiss.

Avery pecked him and stepped safely away, brushing off her clothes. "My mother destroyed my letter before you could get it. I'm sorry you lived so long under the wrong pretenses, but I've made the situation clear to her now."

"I see." He stared at her. "What exactly is clear?"

"That we are no longer engaged."

"I'm not sure that's such a good idea after what's just happened."

Avery froze, seized with panic. "No one knows of this."

"I do. And I'm an honorable man…for the most part."

"You're free and so am I. This is what we both want." Even as she said it, she knew it was a lie.

"Is it truly what you want?"

Before she could retort that she certainly didn't want to be beholden to a man who never bothered to visit, another sound took precedent. The returning of hooves. "I must go. I'm to meet Mary and Campbell at the Tavern. They will be quite worried by now."

"Or ecstatic."

"Regardless. Thank you for your assistance earlier. I regret the villain escaped, but I have other clues. Good day."

"What do you mean you—"

"Shhh!"

Avery left the stall and hurried toward the entrance of the stables. Before she could escape three men escorted the stallions back. One of them was Luc's uncle. "Commodore Rees! Hello."

Avery prayed Luc heard the loud warning. Good lord. If Luc was serious about keeping the betrothal he might humiliate her right now.

"No luck catching your man, Miss Hilfington?"

Avery stared confused, then understood. "No, sir. He got away."

"Where's my nephew? I thought I saw him in pursuit as well."

"We…we…" Avery stared at the man wondering if he knew very well Luc was mere feet from them. "We separated hoping to encircle the villain. I lost the scoundrel, but he must have hidden, for when I passed through the stables the stallions were loosed and nearly ran me down. I was able to take refuge in an open stall."

She hurried toward the street. In another second Luc would be discovered! Then there really would be a betrothal. She looked back.

Commodore Rees walked the opposite direction, casually, handing the reins of a horse to one of the other men. He was going to the stall.

Avery froze, becoming lightheaded in panic. He stopped in front of the stall and stared.

"Miss Hilfington!"

Avery turned around fully, her escape from the stables thwarted. "Y-yes?"

"The evidence tells a different story."

She didn't move. She didn't know what to say, and she wasn't sure how bad this was about to turn out. Slowly she walked back.

To her surprise, the stall was empty, save the little foal. She blinked. The commodore studied the wood shattered about where Luc had kicked it free for them.

"I…I…fell," she explained, before he could surmise differently.

"Indeed. Are you all right?"

"I think so."

He started to step inside.

"Don't go in!"

Commodore Rees turned, curious.

"The uh, foal is quite young and very skittish after the recent…events. And you never know what you might step on in a horses stall hidden innocently by the hay." She checked her own boots as if in warning.

"Nonsense. I'll just remove this wood. Don't want the young thing here getting stabbed accidentally. Then without warning, Commodore Rees stabbed the pile of hay.

Avery gasped in horror. He would uncover Luc!

He stabbed again.

Avery stared, intrigued as Commodore Rees stabbed to no avail.

*Luc was gone.*

"Miss Hilfington!" Luc shouted to her from the entrance of the stables.

*Only not.*

She looked at his silhouette, then back at the stables, wondering. He must have climbed up and slid out the opening at the top left unshielded for circulation. Very clever.

She grinned, as he came running toward her.

"Are you all right?" He huffed out of breath. "I'm sorry. I lost the rascal."

The commodore's brow lifted. "Rascal, indeed."

Luc made a convincing show of observing the broken stall. "Good heavens. He checked her arms and form. Are you injured? What happened?"

"Some stallions chased me down, and I fell in that stall…perhaps I jumped. I was so frightened I hardly remember now. But I left Mary and Campbell, and they must be worried."

"Of course. I will see you to them." He turned to his uncle. "Will you be fine here, Uncle Harry? I'll not be long."

"Humph." Commodore Rees plucked a piece of hay from his nephew's shoulder and studied it. Avery could see the disbelief in his eyes, but they twinkled merrily. "You two," he shook his head. "Haven't changed a bit."

Luc winked at her and offered his arm. "That's where you're wrong, Uncle." Then he leaned in for her ears alone. "Some things have changed quite a bit."

# CHAPTER SIX

Avery made her way down the halls of the naval hospital. The cold interior was at odds with the emotions coursing through her.

They had laughed together.

After the morning's adventure, the kiss, the drama of being caught, the disappointment of losing the watchmaker, and still…walking back to Park Tavern their heads had been together, and they'd laughed like old comrades.

She sighed with regret over her behavior. Not for chasing the watchmaker, but for allowing Luc to kiss her into near oblivion.

He had liked it, certainly, but it was just a matter of time before he left. Had she allowed him to use her? She shook her head, confused. Luc would not use her. He may not care for her enough to actually marry her, but he would not deliberately hurt her.

Then again, she mustn't forget he'd deliberately avoided her for nearly four years, knowing it would hurt her. Perhaps the truth was she didn't know him as well as she thought. They were caught up in the chase this afternoon, and the stallions bearing down on them added fear that made them both react out of character.

*But it had felt so real.*

Her heart ached, while a smile tugged at her lips. It had felt magnificent. The memory made up for the aches in the rest of her body after jumping out a window and being tossed through a horse's stall. But perhaps her feelings were not to be trusted in this matter. The reality so far indicated that Luc did not feel anything similar. Perhaps all this time he'd been trying to protect her? He didn't care for her in the marriage sense but as friend had wanted to protect her pride. Leaving was the best solution. Perhaps he thought she'd be married by now. Her eyes pricked and for a moment the hospital walls closed in on her. It did not bear thinking. And she would accomplish nothing if she fell prey to an emotional storm.

She took a cleansing breath and came back to her task at hand. This afternoon, while Mary and Campbell brought the sailors the benefits of her mother's kitchen, Avery intended to confront Dr. Llewellyn. Now that she had her timepiece and he knew she knew, there seemed no reason to avoid facing the facts. He was a thief.

She knocked on his office door and waited. When there was no response, she looked around, cautious. The halls were relatively quiet. Debating the consequences of her actions, she took out the key she had lifted from the nurse's station yesterday. Turning the lock she pushed open the door, and waited outside.

"Hello? Anyone here? Dr. Llewellyn?"

Curious, Avery stepped inside. Something was different. She walked into the center of the room, turned in a circle, then stopped. She poked her skeleton friend and listened to the hollowed bones. "Well, my friend. It looks like you've been abandoned. Do you come with the office then?"

"Talking to dead people, Avery?"

Avery jumped. Then sighed with relief. "Luc. What are you doing here?"

He frowned. "What are *you* doing *here*? This man stole from you. We don't know the lengths he'll take to get your timepiece back either. And what of the other longitude inventions that have gone missing. Avery, there are at least three men who know what you've been up to and where you live. We don't know how many more there might be or how determined they are. Do you think seeking them out alone is the wisest course of action? What do the authorities say?"

He sounded angry. And condescending.

She straightened her back and reached for the skeleton's bony hand. "Luc, you would benefit from my friend's example and simply remain silent."

"Avery—"

"As you can see from the cleared desk, missing coat, and lack of journals, the mysterious Dr. Llewellyn is gone."

"Good riddance."

Avery tapped her fingers on her lip thinking. Luc interrupted her thoughts again.

"Dear lord," he rushed over to her, taking that same hand. "What in God's name happened?"

Avery looked dispassionately at the cuts on her knuckles. They'd hurt much worse earlier. It wasn't so bad now. "Oh, nothing. It's from punching through the snow earlier. It was fairly hard ice in spots. I should have been wearing my heavy gloves. I hadn't planned on that particular adventure." She put her hands behind her back, away from his worried gaze.

"And yet, you sought out the stable owner."

"You followed me?"

"Of course. You're a lunatic, after all. One can't be too

careful."

"I am not a lunatic! And I don't like that reference. It makes light of my astronomical work and the important work of many others.

"Fine, a longitudinarian."

She scowled. "You're not the least bit affable this afternoon."

"Nonsense. Affable is my middle name."

"Your middle name is Archimedes, which is even more ridiculous. What are *you* doing here anyway?"

"I've come to bring Ned home. The doctor has released him. Mary said you were looking for Llewellyn. I thought you might need…support."

"That's nice of you."

"You're welcome."

"I mean bringing Ned home."

"You're welcome, regardless." He sighed. "Will you join us? He is resisting my assistance."

"If you are trying to carry him, then it's no surprise."

Luc walked straight up to her until they were inches apart. "And you were so sweet this morning."

"You weren't trying to boss me around this morning."

He pecked her on the nose, surprising her. "Come, let us not argue for the duration of Ned's transportation. Then I might have a surprise for you."

She recoiled defensively, her fists tightening. "I think you have surprised me enough for one day."

"From which I gathered that you still like surprises." He smiled slyly, a heavy-hooded gaze warning her that had they not been in a public location earlier, things might have gone further.

She did not want to think about that. It had been a mistake, and she'd be foolish to think a man cared about her, just because he liked kissing her.

"Humph. Let's see how Ned is doing shall we?"

They managed to get Ned into the hands of Luc's mother and her maids—much to his horror. The women were overly solicitous to their modest friend, and Avery was pleased he had so much attention. It would be good for him to be among loved ones during Christmas. He'd had enough holidays alone.

Luc did surprise her by disappearing off to London right after, and if gossip was correct, he did not return that night. It made Avery increasingly irritated and insecure, for she imagined he sought out more amenable female company and titillating pursuits not available in their quiet town. What else was one to imagine?

Early the next day, Campbell and Mary escorted her to the watchmaker's shop, but it was closed and with every villain seeming to be in hiding, Avery returned to a more important task—figuring out how to put her sea watch back together.

Professor Halley had given her a space at the observatory, and she'd begun to separate and meticulously lay out all the finally crafted parts. While the exercise gave her a chance to appreciate her collaborator's work, without the jeweled parts, there was no hope of putting it back together right away. And with Gerrit in Holland, it would be even more difficult.

She rolled her fingers on the table contemplating options. She could send him the design, only the thought of the time wasted seemed excessive. Better to start interviewing craftsmen in London, and do some research. In the meantime, she'd need to find the money for materials—garnet, ruby, sapphire. Perhaps a jeweler could even shape the bearings.

The edges of a rotor pressed the skin of her hand as she turned it, re-envisioning the design, searching for flaws. All the materials would resist rust and humidity, but perhaps it was safer to devise a larger encasement for it. It would be some time before she could retest it on land, let alone the ocean. She'd hoped Luc's uncle could get it tested on one of the king's ships.

Footsteps distracted her from the task of documenting the parts. She lifted the small watch hanging from her neck and checked the time. Fifteen past two. She'd been staring at the pieces of her life for three hours, foregoing luncheon with Campbell, Mary and Halley in hopes of a breakthrough.

Professor Halley joined her in the workroom, followed by Luc and another man. She stared at them curiously, thinking how her telescopic glasses made their heads stretch if she moved suddenly. Remembering that the very same glasses weren't the least bit flattering, and made one's eyes the size of the rotor in her hand, she quickly pulled the strap over her head and laid it on the table, managing to stand politely and keep balance as her eyes adjusted. Luc's lips twitched with amusement, no doubt at catching her in her "longitudinarian" gadgetry. She wanted to make a snappy comment, but simply sighed over the fact that she wasn't nearly as exciting as anything he did last night in London, and there was no changing that.

She turned her attention to the third man, whom she didn't know. He was much older and his shoulders bent forward as if he was accustomed to working over a desk. He nodded to Avery politely but was more interested in the parts displayed before her.

"Miss Hilfington, I'm sorry to disturb you," Luc said. "Your mother told me you were here, and I wanted to introduce Mr. Edward Hargrove. He's a watchmaker from London."

Avery bowed in greeting. That explained the man's interest and perked her own. Perhaps Luc did not taste the delights of London?

Mr. Hargrove lifted one of the gears and studied it. "This *is* Gerrit's work."

"Yes," Avery answered in surprise. He knew her Dutch watchmaker.

He nodded, already affirming it to himself, while pulling out some thick spectacles to inspect further. "Hmm. This might have been some of his best work to date. Shame he returned home."

Avery didn't know what to say to that. She looked to Luc for an explanation.

"I'm hoping Mr. Hargrove can help."

Avery frowned, protective. "I'm not sure. This was a very special project. And you can see how fine the workmanship is." She didn't mean to sound ungrateful or critical, but she wasn't going to let just anybody near her precious instrument—no matter how humble its state.

Hargrove lifted his head and looked at her as if for the first time, pushing his glasses up to give her a proper up and down. Her back stiffened as his eyes stopped on her breasts. He lifted a long, gnarled finger, and pointed at her.

Or her breasts to be exact.

"That," he said. "The lovely timepiece you have there. Tell me about it."

Avery startled. She lifted it, hesitant. Luc had given it to her when she was sixteen. The gift was her most valued possession, in part because it had been from him. "It's a rarity, sir. It keeps more perfect time each day than any instrument I've yet known. It was crafted by H&H Watchmakers, London. But they are no longer in business."

She knew because she had tried to find them to help her.

"Not as H&H," he said, getting her full attention. "I sold that piece to a young, bold lad for a mere song. Never thought I'd see it again." He came closer to her. "May I?" She lifted the watch for him, and he clicked it open expertly. "It was for my daughter. But she passed away birthing my grandson."

"I'm so sorry." Avery choked.

"I think," he said, slowly releasing it. "Still my very best work."

"You made this?"

"Indeed, miss." He looked over his glasses at Luc. "And that boy there convinced me it should belong to only one woman still on earth." He looked down at the pieces organized on the table. "I am gratified that he seems to have been right."

"Thank you, sir. It is indeed a work of art."

He smiled. "Now you flatter me. Come. Tell me what has happened here. Gerrit was my apprentice. I might yet be of help."

Avery was overwhelmed. "I would be most appreciative. I don't know what to say."

"Say 'pull up a chair, Mr. Hargrove,'" Halley suggested.

"Please, pull up a chair, Mr. Hargrove." Avery smiled at him.

The two older men laughed, but Avery thought her heart would explode with affection for Luc. This was his surprise. Indeed it was the most touching and thoughtful act he could have done for her. He'd even brought the man from London.

Their eyes met—his with understanding. She wanted to thank him, hug him, do something. She beamed instead, meeting his blue gaze with gratitude and watching as his own smile grew. The problem now was she did not know what to think—of him, or them, or what the future might hold.

Mr. Hargrove prevented her from worrying about it just then. Halley tugged Luc off for a spot of tea, and Avery sat head to head with the old watchmaker, learning from an expert craftsman just how to rebuild the mechanical device she hoped would help to save many lives in the future, possibly even Luc's.

Luc checked the time. He should start dragging Avery away soon, as he needed to return Mr. Hargrove to London tonight.

"The problem of course," Halley said, "is that magnetic north changes depending where you are in the world. It's no doubt very disconcerting for sailors such as yourself."

"It is a strange phenomenon," Luc agreed.

"I had thought by mapping the variations we'd be closer to a solution on longitude, but alas, years of work and nothing. It seems young Miss Hilfington might get closer than me in the end—and with a mechanical device! So much for science. Not that I mind." He finished his whisky. "Other than the twenty thousand pounds of course." He winked and was about to pour them another round when a feminine laugh caught his attention.

"Speaking of magnetism, boy. Have you worked things out with your betrothed?"

Luc grunted. "Behind the serene face of Venus is a single-minded, stubborn, adventuress. Working things out could take a lifetime."

"Ah, but what a lifetime that would be!"

Luc grinned. "Indeed."

"Chin up. Bringing her Hargrove will go a long way

toward your reconciliation. She looked very kindly on you earlier."

Luc considered that. There had been a moment between them. For a splinter of time she'd been just as he remembered her…when she was fond of him. But would he have enough time to truly win her heart before he told her his decision about his future? And would she choose him over more secure circumstances?

Avery finally joined them.

"Lieutenant Rees, I'm sorry, Mr. Hargrove tells me you are returning him to London this afternoon. I didn't mean to keep him so late."

Her face glowed with energy and excitement. For a moment, Luc could not tear his gaze away. She was pleased indeed! Her eyes fell on him kindly and his entire body relaxed for the first time in several days.

"It was a productive afternoon then?"

"Oh, yes!" She and Hargrove turned to each other nodding. "Very!"

Halley gave him a sly nod of encouragement. "Excellent! Perhaps our young man here is not so dimwitted after all. I've hopes for you yet my boy. Don't you agree, Miss Hilfington?"

The group waited for Avery's agreement. Instead, she tilted her head at him, considering. "Well…he has certainly shown some portion of good sense and kindness in bringing Mr. Hargrove to my aid."

Luc nodded his thanks humbly and Avery relented, a brilliant expression overcoming her.

"Truly, I am inordinately grateful."

"It is the least an old friend can do," Luc said.

"Indeed," Halley said.

"Indeed," Avery and Luc agreed simultaneously.

"Alas, we must away." Luc bowed his farewell to the old

astronomer. "Miss Hilfington, I'll drop you and your chaperones at home on my way if you'll allow me." On cue, Mary and Campbell ensconced in the corner, stood to leave.

"Yes, but I want to sit up top. I need the fresh air."

Luc could not have thought of a better idea. He helped Avery to the carriage seat next to him, while Hargrove, Mary and Campbell settled inside.

"Guess what else?" She leaned into him, and spoke with a confidential whisper, excited to share something more.

Luc's stomach flipped in eager excitement—not merely from the promise of adventure on her face, but the fact that she confided in him, an honor he'd not had in three years, eleven months and eight days.

"What?" he whispered back, lowering his head to hers.

"Mr. Hargrove knows every watchmaker in London and Greenwich."

"Indeed."

"Indeed!" she said, excitement growing. "There are two watchmakers of note in Greenwich—Williams and Horace. I've met both, but neither has the talent of Mr. Hargrove."

"I know."

"You know?"

"When I purchased your watch, I investigated my options thoroughly."

"Oh." She blinked and stared. Then blinked again. "I did not know you put so much thought into the gift." She touched his arm lightly before pulling away. "It is even more precious now. Thank you, Luc."

"You're welcome."

"How is it you turned into such a clod right after giving it to me?"

He shrugged helplessly. "Men are clods."

"Indeed," she agreed.

"Indeed," he sighed with apology. "But we digress. The watchmakers."

She was about to continue when Campbell stuck his head out. "Everything a'right up there, Miss Hilfington?"

They had yet to move. Avery called back that all was well, and Luc gently pulled the reins to take them home. He turned to Avery and asked her to continue. She had to speak louder for him to hear over the horses' hooves.

"In addition to Williams and Horace, there was a third master craftsman."

"Was?" He sensed a word of warning might be in order.

"Yes!" she said gleefully. "He's dead!"

"Probably best not to delight in the misfortunes of others," he commented.

"I know. But I did not kill him. In fact he was not killed at all, which is less exciting, but passed away from a heart ailment of some sort. May he rest in peace."

"Amen."

"The interesting part—"

"That was all very interesting."

"Yes, but there is more—guess what his name was?"

She waited. Luc turned his head briefly to see her waiting expectantly, as if he should know the answer. Damn. He did not want to disappoint her but who could follow the relevance of this information. There were very few clues for him to grasp onto. One clicked, and he took a stab.

"Llewellyn?"

"Yes!" She grabbed his arm excitedly, and a thrill of relief washed through him—followed by concern. "What is the connection?"

"It seems, according to watchmaker rumors, that Llewellyn's brother was also working on a device to solve longitude, long before the Longitude Act. When he passed away, his family found his work, but no one really understood his thinking. Hargrove believes his brother, the doctor, has been trying to understand the devices. He may have stolen mine to compare, or to stop me, I don't know that part. But Llewellyn's widow, that is the watchmaker's widow, still lives in Greenwich. I'm going to call on her!"

With that final announcement, Avery turned forward in her seat. He glanced down making a quick study of her resolute expression and knew discussion was out of the question.

"I'll bring you."

"You will?"

"Indeed. If you will wait for me to return Hargrove. We can visit the widow Llewellyn tomorrow."

"You don't need to, you know. I'm sure it's perfectly safe."

He gave her a very deliberate and skeptical look. "I'm sure you thought that when you called on the good doctor, and the stable hand."

She smirked, and turned her head away. "I was prepared."

They stopped in front of her home, and Luc hurried to assist her, welcoming the slide of her body against his, before he stepped away. Campbell helped Mary to the ground. Luc caught sight of Avery's mother in the window. She waved. He lifted his hand in return before catching Avery's. She was about to run off. Instead he pulled her gently toward him.

"Humor me, and do nothing until I can accompany you, Avery."

She didn't say anything, but tried to release her hand. He held firm.

He squeezed her hand. "Promise," he insisted.

She pulled again, but he stood unyielding. He could be as stubborn as her about some things and her safety was one of them.

She glanced up and both saw her mother watching them. Avery reluctantly acquiesced. "Very well, but don't dally in London."

Her eyes showed a hint of suspicion, as if she did not trust him alone in London. A light of understanding sunk in. She was jealous.

He lifted her hand slowly to his lips, maintaining contact with her dark wary eyes, and caressed his thumb over a glove-encased knuckle. Still holding her hand, he confessed. "I never dally in London, Avery. Not when the most interesting entertainments are here in Greenwich."

"But there are no entertainments in Greenwich!"

He squeezed her hand gently when she didn't understand. "You do yourself great injustice, my love."

"Oh." A smile tickled her lips, and her eyes sparkled with delighted surprise.

"Tomorrow then," he confirmed, satisfied she could be confident of his regard.

She nodded. "Tomorrow." Then she reached out most unexpectedly and gave him an exuberant hug. "Thank you again for bringing Hargrove to me. Godspeed, Luc." She tapped the door of the carriage. "Farewell for now, Mr. Hargrove. And Merry Christmas! We shall meet again after the holiday."

"Merry Christmas to you too, Miss Hilfington. I shall look forward to our next affair. Perhaps your young man will bring you to my shop in London."

"I would love that, Mr. Hargrove."

They waved farewell and Luc launched into the driver's seat, his energy renewed. He would happily bring Avery to London…with their mothers of course. There was no way around that. He grinned at the thought, taking the reins, while he followed her steps to the door. He waited.

*Turn around, my love. Don't let me leave you without a fond farewell. There have been too many without you.*

The door opened. Before entering she turned. And then the most beautiful woman in all of England smiled and waved farewell.

# CHAPTER SEVEN

Avery ducked another swipe from the hairbrush, barely avoiding her mother's urgent strokes. "Mother, please! Stop fussing," Avery took the offending brush. "We are going for chocolate, not to Windsor Castle."

"Well, I don't see why you could not have worn your red dress. It's Christmas Eve after all, and red looks so spectacular on you." Without a brush to hold, her mother started turning over hourglasses on Avery's vanity. Avery had another collection of them on her table by the window. She put the brush down there, next to her father's compass and sextant.

"I'm wearing red tonight for the ball. Blue is very wintry as well." Avery snatched a warm cloak from the wardrobe. "Mary, are you ready?"

"Yes, miss. My cloak is by the door downstairs."

"I saw how he looked at you yesterday?"

"Who?" Avery did not want to have this conversation with her mother.

"You know who. Luc!" She fluffed the bottom of Avery's long dark hair. "I believe he might be done with the sea. His mother wishes him to stay home. Not that what a mother wants *ever* seems to matter to our children."

"All children are ungrateful." Avery kissed her mother on the cheek. "A fair warning to women to not have children at all."

"Oh! I didn't mean that. I should like to have some grandchildren."

"I thought all this time you wanted me married. If you only want grandchildren, that's simple enough."

Her mother smacked her playfully on the behind and Mary laughed. "Do not even consider that. It just seems that you and Luc have patched things up. And you both seem happy, so I'm happy too. That is enough. And we will all be together for Christmas."

Avery nodded. She was happy this Christmas too. Luc was here. Their families would be together. And for once there would be someone at the Christmas ball tonight that she wanted to dance with. The thought of turning about the dance floor in Luc's arms, moving together to music— she sighed happily—suddenly the future held such promise.

"Come along, and say a quick hello." Knowing her mother, she stopped in the doorway with a mock stern face, and emphasized, "*Quick.*"

"Honestly, you've no faith in my womanly discretion."

The three women went downstairs, and Mary joined Campbell while Avery's mother floated into the front sitting room to greet Luc.

"My dear, Luc. Or must I call you Sir Luc?" She grasped his hands affectionately.

"Anything other than Luc would be unnatural."

She smiled and released him. "I'm looking forward to tonight. The Astin ball has not been the same without you. Avery is always promised within minutes of arriving, but I know we will be able to find you plenty of partners."

Avery nearly laughed. Luc remained unfazed, but eyed

her mother wolfishly.

"I hoped only to dance with you Mrs. Hilfington. If I can thwart my dear uncle. Your name seems to be on his lips quite often of late."

To Avery's surprise her mother blushed. This was news. Goodness, had she had her head buried in her own life so long that she had not seen a relationship? And how did she feel about that?

"Your uncle is a charming man, but I will save the first set for you." Her mother seemed to think that was enough conversation for she ushered them out the door with surprising speed, befuddling Avery even further. Was her mother interested in Harry Rees?

Before she could consider if further, Luc squeezed her hand for attention, and helped her into the carriage.

"You look lovely as usual." He kissed her forehead. "Merry Christmas Eve."

Avery warmed under his appreciation. "Thank you. Merry Christmas Eve to you too!"

"It's too cold this morning for up top. There are blankets inside to keep you warm."

"Thank you," she said again, and climbed in with Mary. "Luc?"

He came back to her. "I told my mother we were going for chocolate."

He nodded understanding. "And so we will. After we meet with the Widow Llewellyn." He held up a scrap of parchment. "Uncle Harry was useful in uncovering her residence. It is a short drive across town, and then we will have chocolate. Will that meet with you approval?"

She nodded, grinning. "Yes. Thank you. Again."

Avery leaned back in the carriage seat as he closed the door.

"He looks on you the way Campbell looks on me," Mary

said.

"We are old friends. It is different," Avery said.

Mary nodded and said nothing more, but during the short drive, Avery couldn't stop the feeling of hope in her heart that it was something more.

Mrs. Llewellyn, wife of deceased watchmaker Bernard Llewellyn, was cautious when they knocked on her door. After Avery shared her interest in longitude the woman nearly burst with chatter, revealing it was an ongoing hobby of her late husband's to tinker on devices that might allow England to tell time at sea.

"Please come in. I have kept all of Bernard's projects in the hopes some day they might be of value."

Their home was above his former workshop, now rented to a cobbler. They climbed up the narrow steps single file, into a small but comfortable family compartment. The furniture was simple but well looked after.

"Just one more floor. We converted the attic. Watch your heads," Mrs. Llewellyn suggested to Luc. "You too, miss. I've hit mine enough times."

They entered the attic and found a small bed with several makeshift desks around the edge of the room filled with contraptions—some complete, some in process.

"My brother-in-law stays in this room on occasion. I keep all Bernard's projects in here."

"Dr. Llewellyn works at the hospital, does he not?" Luc asked courteously, engaging her with a smile that could melt snow.

Mrs. Llewellyn responded with eager surprise, then understanding. "Why, yes! But of course you'd know. I hope you've not had need of his services, Lieutenant Rees."

"No, ma'am, but many of my friends have. It's a valued profession, as was the work your husband engaged in. If any of his inventions could solve longitude, there would be many families who would be grateful beyond words."

The sincerity and significance of Luc's words brought pinpricks of moisture to Avery's eyes, and the widow did not miss it.

"You've suffered a loss already," she said.

"My father," Avery said. In oh-seven—" Her throat tightened, making it impossible to speak of the horrific loss of lives off the Scilly Islands in 1707. She'd been devastated by the tragedy, and Luc had been the only one who could reach her emotionally afterward. He'd been her anchor, reminding how to play and laugh again, for she'd been only a child. In some ways, his understanding of her pain had made it doubly hurtful when he'd left to go to sea. She'd cursed him many a night, listing in her mind the many other options he had instead of the navy. Even now, it made her angry with him.

"So many were lost," the woman sympathized. "It touched everyone in Greenwich. I always thought here more so than anywhere else. Bernard had been tinkering long before then, but it seemed to spur everyone on even more. His youngest brother was lost as well."

"Oh! I'm so sorry."

The widow reached for her hand. "His brothers were close. Of late, Bradford has become equally hopeful of a solution."

"You understand my interest then, but I don't want to intrude on your privacy."

"Nonsense." She looked around the chamber as if to make sure it was fit for visitors. "Bradford is out at the moment, but said he would return tonight to spend Christmas with us. He's moving to Dartford now that

Bernard's gone, and we might join him eventually."

A youthful male voice called for his mother and Mrs. Llewellyn said she would be right there. "Sorry, he's watching the biscuits for me."

"They smell wonderful. Pumpkin biscuits are a favorite of mine, I don't blame him for guarding the oven judiciously," Luc said.

Mrs. Llewellyn laughed in response. "I shall send you home with some."

"You are too generous, ma'am."

Honestly, Luc was an incorrigible flirt. Avery turned the topic back to one of her interest. "You said Dr. Llewellyn is in town?"

"Yes. I shall tell him you called. He might be a better guide to Bernard's work than myself."

"Oh, that's not—"

"Mum!" A warning called again from below.

"That would be wonderful," Luc cut in. "Thank you."

"Of course," Mrs. Llewellyn smiled. "My apologies, may I leave you for just a moment?"

"Please," Avery said. "We're the ones who arrived so unexpectedly."

The woman left and Avery turned to Luc, befuddled. "This is not at all what I expected."

"Indeed." He strolled to the table where numerous devices, large and small were displayed. "Yet here we are. And here is also where the devious Dr. Llewellyn could be laying in wait."

"Maybe he is not so devious as I first thought."

"Yes," Luc agreed. "The mystery takes an odd turn."

Avery took a fortifying breath, and turned to the more personal area of the room—the chamber drawers.

"What are you doing?" Luc asked.

"Investigating. Go through the desk against the wall,

please. And hurry."

Luc grinned mischievously but obeyed. "I feel dastardly, but excited."

"I know," she whispered.

Avery made quick work of sliding her hands underneath clothes and through the standing wardrobe. She didn't know what she would find, only that if a clue existed she intended to uncover it. A lightning-fast survey revealed nothing until Avery flipped through the two journals by the bedside. There was a paper folded inside the pages of one. She pulled it out, truly expecting nothing, until she saw her name listed.

"Luc," she gasped.

"What is it?"

Avery read the list quickly, Dr. Llewellyn's guilt cemented in her mind. It was a list of navigational devices and materials, many which had been stolen in the last six months.

The footsteps on the wood staircase sounded Mrs. Llewellyn's return. Avery's heart pounded in indecision.

"Put it back," Luc motioned.

Avery shook her head. Luc glanced at the doorway. Only a few more steps. Still uncertain of his advice, Avery turned her back on him and flipped the pages of the book before hurrying over to the device table behind her.

Luc pretended to point. "That's an ingenious bit of work there."

"Indeed," Avery said. At a loss to know what she was looking at, as the contraption made no sense to her, she added, "And very finely crafted."

"That is everyone's favorite," Mrs. Llewellyn said, smiling at them.

Avery thought she would rot in hell for deceiving an innocent widow on Christmas Eve. It did not bear thinking. Yet there was another injustice taking place, and something about that list tickled her brain. She just didn't know what it was yet.

They continued to look at the devices with Mrs. Llewellyn. Avery was imminently grateful for Luc's presence and the way he easily chatted up the widow. She made good on her word and sent him off with four warm pumpkin biscuits. He insisted he could not deny her son more than that. After he raised her hand to his lips, Avery thought he would have a source of pumpkin biscuits for life.

At the same time, Avery could not find it in her to dislike the woman for she had been kind and gracious, and she was lonely after losing a man she clearly loved and admired. It had been in her every word, and the way she wanted to show off his life's work. And it made this conundrum even more problematic, for the lines of good and evil had suddenly become not so good and not so evil—with Avery feeling in the not-so-good category.

She thought of the document stealthily stowed in her hand purse. Luc would not approve, she was certain.

Luc and Avery reached the carriage, but when Avery stepped up, what she saw inside made her stumble back in surprise. Luc handily caught her in his arms.

"Are you unharmed?"

Avery nodded, biting her lip. She did not know whether to laugh or not, for she had inadvertently discovered Campbell and Mary in a compromising embrace. Not that she had any illusions about their attraction, she had in fact, enabled them. And considering how Luc was holding her right now, she could in no way condemn Mary for embracing the man she loved. It was actually rather wonderful. Her heart pounded under the intensity of Luc's hot blue gaze, and her lips throbbed in anticipation when his eyes wandered to them, as if being drawn to kiss her right there and then against his better judgment. A fuss in the carriage prevented it.

Campbell came around to them, and Avery tapped Luc to release her. He didn't.

"Miss Hilfington, Sir Luc," he started, his face bright red. "It is not what you think."

Luc tilted his head curiously. "I did not think anything. Avery? Did you?"

"Why no. I slipped from the ice on the carriage lift, and clumsily fell back."

"But I caught you."

"Much to my relief."

"You're welcome," Luc said.

"You may release me now."

He ignored her.

Campbell nodded, looking relieved. "It gives me great joy to tell you I have asked Mary to be my wife, and she has agreed."

"Indeed!" Luc dropped her on the ground and left her to fumble for her balance. "Fantastic news, my good man." He slapped Campbell on the back and pumped his hand vigorously. "She's a fine woman."

"Yes, sir. She is."

Mary peeked out, and Luc reached for her hand as well. "Marvelous news, Mary."

"Yes, it is." Avery smiled warmly. "I thought you would propose over chocolate, so I am surprised but thrilled."

"He couldn't wait!" Mary said, blushing with pleasure. She lifted a necklace with a gold charm shaped into a heart. "He gave me this as a promissory token."

Avery admired it. "It's lovely, Mary. I'm so happy for you." And she was, which was why the unaccountable tears that came to her eyes were such surprise. This day was becoming quite emotional. Mary's eyes became watery as well. "It would not have happened without your kindness, Miss Hilfington."

"Nonsense," Avery said. "Campbell would have come around eventually." Then she teased. "I just made him pay attention sooner than he planned."

"That's the right of it!" Campbell said. "I'd no intention of taking a wife so young, but I couldn't let her pass by."

The four of them laughed on the damp roadside and it wasn't until another carriage rolled by that Avery realized it was not the best place for a celebration. "I think champagne is in order. And we must share the news."

"Am I invited?" Luc asked.

"Of course!" Avery said. "Unless you are above champagne in my mother's kitchen."

"I love your mother's kitchen. It was my favorite place to hide at your home."

At Campbell's surprised look, Avery clarified. "It was long ago, and we were not even seven. Hiding and seeking was good fun then. Especially if it involved sneaking goodies from Cook. Though, of course, it turns out she knew all along."

Luc nodded. "Good memories. Let's make some more, shall we."

The four returned to the Hilfington household for an impromptu celebration. Avery was eager to get home as well. She wished to inspect her latest clue, and that would not be possible until secure in the privacy of her own room. She'd been targeted by whomever had written up the list, and she intended to find out why.

Luc topped off Mrs. Hilfington's and Cook's champagne

before adding to his own. The morning had turned into a casual luncheon celebration, and he found himself enjoying the time, catching up with a few of the older members of Avery's household who knew him as a boy. They had no qualms about sharing stories of his and Avery's childhood mischief, some of the mischief involving sneaking provisions from the kitchen—very important work back then.

"Aye, you were two peas in a pod," Rufus, the old butler said.

"Until you left us all," Constance Hilfington said. "With nary a farewell."

There was a chorus of grumbled agreement.

"A man's gotta learn what he's made of, ma'am," Rufus defended. "And we all know Avery would have tied him up in a closet had she learned his plans."

The others laughed, but the truth of the words made Luc look for Avery's reaction. She could make him do anything for her. And when she couldn't, she played dirty. That's what he loved about her. It was always an even fight.

"Where did she go?" Luc asked.

"She went to get something in her room. Will you get her, Luc?" Mrs. Hilfington requested. "Tell her we are ready to eat luncheon, and it will be a long time before Christmas supper."

"Yes, ma'am."

Luc jumped to run the errand and he didn't care who noticed. He nearly kissed Avery's mother with gratitude. The entire household was crowded in the kitchen, which meant he would have Avery to himself for a few minutes, and with her mother's permission. That was a Christmas gift all on its own. There were a few knowing laughs. He had perhaps jumped too quickly.

"I'll be counting the seconds, young man!" Mrs.

Hilfington called after him.

"Yes, ma'am!"

Luc found Avery as her mother suspected—in her room. The door was closed halfway, and he quietly pushed it open to find Avery standing by the windowsill, a paper in her hand, surrounded by all the things that were infinitely Avery—her time pieces and compasses, the map of the stars, the landscape of Greenwich with a host of ships in the Thames. She had a view to the observatory from her window and he fancied she still dreamt one day there would be a female Astronomer Royal. The wood of the furnishings was as dark as her hair with only blue in the blankets and cushions to soften the severity of the room.

He leaned against the doorway, taking in the moment. She looked familiar, yet different. She'd become more of a mystery to him with age and time. He would never know all of her, but he loved the thought of finding out.

She had continued her life, pursuing knowledge and adventure, just as they had always sworn to do—only he had left her to do it on her own, and he on his own. Rufus had it right. He needed to know what he was made of and if any of it was good enough for Avery. They'd both lived modest lives upon the passing of their fathers and despite having a barely solvent baronetcy, Luc had little to offer her. How did a man explain that and still keep his pride?

She put the paper in a box on the side table. "It's snowing. It will be a very white Christmas."

She'd been aware of him.

"You like white Christmases."

She nodded, looking out the window, her back tensing. "Are you spying on me, Luc?"

"Not at all. Enjoying the view. I have missed this one sorely in the last four years."

Avery spun and shook her head disbelieving, her eyes

guarded.

"There is no one about. You needn't impress me."

"And yet I want to," he said, entering the room and joining her by the window. "Every time I see you, I am more and more in awe that I could have left you for even one day."

"And yet," she paused to make her point, "you did."

"Yes." He added, to clarify his position, "I'm not sorry for it, Avery."

"How nice for you."

Luc didn't miss the hurt in her eyes. It cut him to think of her alone and wondering about his departure, but at the time, he'd not had a better solution. He took another step closer. He wanted to tell her the truth. "Not particularly. Sea life can be utterly boring. But there is plenty of time for a man to think about his choices in life, and regret the bad ones."

"You don't owe me an explanation." She started to make for the door. He stopped her.

"My mother will be expecting me."

"Your mother sent me. And she surely knew my intentions."

Avery's eyes widened, curious. "And what are those?"

"To ravish you, of course."

She stepped back defensively, startled. Recovering, she laughed. Nervously, he noted.

He took another step forward, and before she could retreat, he snatched her around the waist and pulled her to him. She leaned away, her hands on this chest, her hips pressing enticingly into his.

"Yes, that feels nice."

Color flushed her cheeks. "We cannot do this."

"In the stables, I believe you said you wanted to do this more."

"I was overcome by the gaseous odor of horse manure!"

A hoot of laughter escaped him. He grinned wickedly and teased her further.

"I think," he leaned in to breathe along the slender side of her neck, "you were overcome by the rapture of my kisses."

She laughed harder. "Stop. You are being ridiculous now. And you're a terrible tease!"

"Oh?" He lifted his head, fixing his eyes on hers, warning. "I think you may be assured of one thing, my love." His free hand glided gently across the softness of her chest, eliciting a traitorous gasp. "I am most definitely, *not* teasing."

He lowered his mouth slowly to hers.

"Luc," she said, her voice uncertain but her eyes closing in welcome.

"Indeed," he said against her lips. "I am." He pulled her more securely around the waist until he knew she could feel every muscle in his body, and understand it was her that he needed. Above all things, it had always been her.

The fingers of his right hand slid up the delicate and delicious skin near her throat, then up and across her jaw, before threading through thick waves of hair. He captured her and controlled her, making her wait, all the while knowing she hated to wait. He leaned his cheek to graze hers, tantalizing, patient. She still resisted him. He knew her well enough to know that—even if her body was pliant in his arms.

He breathed in her scent. The scent of heaven. Again he brushed his lips across hers barely touching.

"Is this the ravishing part?" she asked.

Luc smiled. She opened hooded eyes, revealing an intensity of hunger that prevailed over all polite inclinations he might have held onto. It had been too long. This was what they had always been meant for, and he wouldn't wait any longer.

"No, my love." He took a final breath, his control lost. "This is."

# CHAPTER EIGHT

Ravishing felt…wonderful!

His mouth possessed her, sensuous, gliding, tasting. She tasted back, enjoying the hint of champagne, the heat that burned her cool lips, and the feeling of his desire pressed against her. It made her feel aware, alive, and surprisingly powerful.

Avery's hands slid to his arms for balance, only to find hard muscle that defied her grip. A thrill of awareness darted through her palms and spread a tingling sensation through her body. It would be a mistake to underestimate his strength. She pushed against his chest, testing, but he held firm, an immovable object except those lips…

A moan of pleasure escaped. Avery glided her hands through his thick hair and wrapped her arms around his neck, not just surrendering but claiming. She wanted this. His hand moved easily up her side until she felt his thumb graze her breast. Then he reversed and stopped, moving it over a nipple, taut through her clothing. Back and forth, he tormented until she cried out with frustration and gripped his hair to yank him from her.

Heavy lids lifted partially to reveal his brilliant blue eyes, hot with desire and determination. "I want you."

"We can't. The others—"

"Are all in the kitchen drinking champagne and enjoying a meal. They won't notice another moment…or two."

She desperately wanted to believe that.

He reached and flipped the first hourglass on her bedside table, negotiating. "Just two minutes." He took another look at her, his expression hungry, and flipped the second hourglass. "Make that five."

A second later his lips descended and they devoured each other, hungry to feed the emptiness of so much time apart. Avery arched with abandon when his lips left her mouth to trace a tantalizing path toward her breasts. He gently tugged and released the thin material tucked there earlier for modesty and dropped it on the floor. His growl of approval squashed any inhibition she might have had. His free hand slid down her back and over her buttocks, the sudden grip caused her to gasp, then clutch securely as he lifted her, and laid her on the bed. She pulled at his hair, her knee arching to enfold him through her heavy skirts. Things she had never dreamed of doing she now imagined enjoying. Through a haze of pleasure she realized life continued to educate her in surprising ways. How marvelous.

She smiled blissfully as Luc's hot breath sizzled over her chest. He inched the material lower while she waited, savoring the silky feel of his lips gradually reaching their goal. She released an appreciative sigh of pure joy.

"Ahhh…"

"Choo!"

Avery froze. Luc looked up at her response.

"Ah-choo!"

It came from down the hall. Luc came to his senses first. He regained his feet and yanked Avery to hers with such speed she nearly lost her balance. Avery grabbed the first knick-knack off the table near her for a plausible diversion and looked down as if studying it. It took her a moment to register her father's old compass.

"It still points north," she remarked inanely as the footsteps reached her door. She looked up. "Oh, hello, Mother."

"My dears. Come have a bite"—she seemed to pause pointedly in Avery's guilty mind—"to eat."

"Of course," Luc said. "We got distracted."

Her mother raised a brow and Avery rushed to explain, lifting the compass.

"We were debating the virtues of magnetic north versus true north."

"Indeed," Luc agreed.

"And what was the consensus?"

"True."

"Magnetic." They both said the opposite at once.

Avery turned to him with surprise, only to notice her compass wasn't the only thing pointing north. Heat rushed over her, and Luc casually stepped behind the table and toward the window.

"Well, it seems you don't agree. Not to worry, you will have plenty of time over the holiday season to debate the merits of each, won't you Luc?"

"Indeed," Luc said, surprising Avery further.

Tension she'd been unaware of suddenly released from her body. Her mother had gained information that Luc was here to stay, at least for a while. Relief flooded her, followed by an attack of happiness that began to fill her entire being with optimism. Luc did indeed want to mend things, and this…well, this unaccountable converging of bodies was perhaps not that of a scoundrel, but of a man who genuinely cared, and intended to follow up honorably.

She would never make him do that, but at the same time she did not think Luc would take advantage of her. Hadn't his every action in the last few days indicated he cared?

She caught his eyes again, and this time his smile was gentle. Maybe even loving?

Her heart warmed, not that her temperature wasn't hot enough, but he touched a different part of her with that look. Her mother's hand caught the compass and put it on the table. Yes, even her mother smiled at the exchange.

"Come along, you two. Commodore Rees has joined our celebration."

They followed her mother below, and Avery, now completely in charge of her capacities, observed her mother taking the offered arm of the Commodore at the bottom of the stairs. She didn't miss the stern searching look he gave Luc, but Avery was more curious about the look he turned on her mother.

He had always seemed a charming scoundrel and flirt, but there was a possessive quality to his gaze suddenly laid bear on her mother. Avery's back stiffened in sudden awareness and surprise.

Her mother's response was reserved and polite, her comportment one of genteelness. She was still a very beautiful woman. Few lines marred her skin, and her figure was as trim as when Avery was a child. Likely men would find her intriguing and attractive, aside from her lack of funds. Avery had never thought too much of it. They had always gotten by well enough, and keeping a small staff helped. Commodore Rees was a weathered man of the sea, fit for his age and bearing the blue eyes of the Rees men. Where she had thought him old, she reassessed. Though his dark hair mixed with white at the temples, he was perhaps younger than his seasoned face revealed. She tried to imagine Luc in twenty years, and suddenly his Uncle

Harry did not seem old and jovial, but sharp-eyed and dangerous. Thinking of Luc's restrained strength earlier, she recognized with some discomfort that his uncle displayed a similar physique. Was it one that attracted her mother?

"It doesn't bear thinking." Avery closed her eyes to recover from the onslaught of her imagination.

"What doesn't?" Luc whispered behind her.

She'd mumbled aloud. How inconvenient. "Nothing."

"It seemed something."

"It's not. Go away."

"I cannot. My compass is magnetically drawn to you," he murmured for her ears only.

"Perhaps it needs to be recalibrated," Avery said, coolly.

"If you are doing the tuning, I will submit willingly."

Avery spun, unable to maintain a stern expression in face of his fiendish wink and smile. "Do stay away, Luc, or I shall likely end up slapping you most unwittingly."

"It will be well-deserved, I'm sure," Commodore Rees interrupted them.

They both straightened their backs and assumed a more appropriate expression of decorum and pleasantness.

"Uh-hmm. Well much better. Let us eat and celebrate shall we." Commodore Rees waved them ahead.

"Excellent plan, Uncle Harry."

Avery nodded to both men, then promptly went to assist serving the casual buffet the household shared in, with Mary and Campbell at the center of the festivities. Soon everyone would be napping after food and drinks, and she'd be able to sneak out once again to check on the latest clue. Llewellyn's list was detailed. There were two items that she knew had not yet been stolen and one that she needed to confirm. It would be a simple matter to handle before anyone even noticed her missing. She checked her timepiece. Yes, it was still very early. Perhaps she would even have a nap her herself. She felt Luc's regard and instinctively turned. Alone, she would nap alone. He raised his glass to her.

Then again, this was turning out to be such an amusing Christmas Eve, napping seemed a wasted endeavor. There would be plenty of time to sleep tomorrow. Today was hers.

The impromptu celebration had gone on longer than expected, but had been remarkably enjoyable. An afternoon of food, wine, and friends was indeed the best way to spend one's time.

Luc pulled his collar up against the chill, wishing for a warm fire and a long nap.

His uncle looked like he felt the same. "Tell me again, why we're waiting in the park behind a tree ready to dump snow on us?" The commodore puffed smoke from his cigar in an effort to stay warm.

"A hunch."

"I see." His uncle inhaled the tobacco and released a spicy aroma. "How long before we decide it wasn't a hunch?"

It had been nearly half an hour. Perhaps he was wrong.

"Avery checked her timepiece three times."

"Four," Harry corrected.

"You see." Luc was not surprised his uncle noticed. "She's up to something."

"And you intend to find out?"

"Someone must protect her. She's become obsessed, I'm afraid."

"With longitude."

"What else."

"Can you blame her? Her father died in Scilly, her mother never stopped mourning, and her best friend abandoned her for the sea. No doubt she seeks some measure of control." He puffed out a circle of smoke rings.

Luc picked up on the most important nuance. "No luck with Mrs. Hilfington?"

"None."

He slapped his uncle on the back with humor.

His uncle puffed another ring in the air and poked his finger through it. "Yet, I can't seem to help myself from trying."

"That's the curse of it, isn't it?"

Harry laughed. "Don't let them hear you say that."

"God forbid." Just when he thought it might be time for a stiff drink, his prey showed her face. She came from the back entrance out the narrow passage between homes. Her clothes where all black with a black cloak and hood covering her, much like the day he'd encountered her at the hospital. "The vixen! What is she up to? And why didn't she invite me?"

Luc was about to step out and follow, when his uncle's hand darted out and stopped him.

"Wait."

A man in a worn, dark suit got up from a bench and started to walk the same direction.

"He's following her," Luc said.

"So it seems." Harry frowned.

"Who is he?"

"I don't know."

Luc raised a brow, surprised. "You know everyone."

Harry shrugged. "He must be new in town."

Not expecting this, Luc lifted his feet out of the deep snow, prepared to follow. He looked back at his uncle.

"Are you coming?"

Harry stared at the Hilfington house thoughtfully and shook his head. "He's a small man. I think you can handle it alone." Then he winked. "Avery is another thing altogether."

Luc's body still burned with the memory of her responding in his arms. He gave his uncle a wry grin. "You speak the truth, Uncle Harry."

This time his uncle slapped him on the back. "I'll see you at home. Though I suspect he is only meant to gather information, don't underestimate him."

Luc nodded and hurried to follow. Damn Avery. He couldn't be everywhere at once. Who would protect her when he wasn't around? He was having enough trouble doing it when he was here.

He followed as she turned toward the river. A knot formed in his gut. The thought of her in that part of town, no matter how many people she knew, did not bode well.

The man following her picked up his pace, clearly thinking she made an easy victim.

He was about to learn otherwise.

Their journey was short. The villain following Avery kept a safe distance once he realized where she was going—the magistrate's office. For once she showed good sense.

Luc waited, leaning casually against the cold stone of a building on the corner. He rubbed his gloved hands for warmth. He didn't imagine there were many around Christmas Eve to help.

She came back outside, her face serious and thoughtful as if deciding her next move. After a moment, she pulled her hood up for warmth, or perhaps to cover her face. He didn't think as a disguise it worked, but it made her less noticeable among the general street vendors and goings on.

The man shadowing moved from down the block and followed at a safe distance. Luc ducked into a doorway as both passed by him.

Avery walked toward the water, along the riverbank, and stared for a while at the ships. There were various food vendors hawking their business under a makeshift tent and she bought a small bag of nuts from a raggedy kid whose mother roasted them over a small fire. After tasting one, she ordered several more bags, much to the child's delight. She exchanged words and money with the mother, and just when she was about to wander on, the woman called her back.

Luc saw a quick change in Avery's body language. She nodded to the woman, and after a moment, slowly looked around until she identified the man following her. He acted as if he was interested in a display of hats one might find on a working sailor. Something told Luc he was no sailor. And judging by Avery's inability to hide her distress, she would make a miserable spy.

With a disturbing suddenness, Avery disappeared between vendors. Luc's heart caught. Damn, the woman could move fast. The man following launched into the heart of the marketplace after her.

Luc studied the scene. There was nothing the man could do in public…right? He hurried around the outer edge of the tent following Avery's clumsy progress between startled vendors. If he estimated correctly she'd exit right into his arms. He could see her bobbing head coming toward him even now.

A startled squeal made chills run up his spine. Luc saw her face, but she did not see him. The villain must have pulled her cloak. She turned and struggled.

"Avery!"

Avery spun back toward him, off balance, but at the

edge of the tent. She reached out wildly so as not to fall, her hand grasping at a barrel.

Her bag of roasted nuts went flying as her body twisted. Luc went to catch her under the arms, but her bottom knocked him backward, and they both tumbled to the ground. Unfortunately, the barrel Avery had been reaching for went with them, launching its contents.

Avery screamed as a hundred little fish, kept fresh with snowy water, spilled into their laps.

# CHAPTER NINE

Free of their captivity, fish began desperately wiggling and flopping about. Fortunately, Luc had Avery to shield him from the worst. Damned if she didn't deserve it.

There was shocked silence followed by a burst of laughter and then shouts from a very disgruntled fishmonger. Avery tossed a fish from her skirts and Luc felt her shudder of disgust against his body.

He managed to slide her off his legs and get to his feet before offering a hand.

"Luc? What are you doing here?"

She accepted the hand and took a couple of wobbly steps toward the tent, looking for her pursuer, but Luc held her back.

"Let's not discuss that yet," he suggested.

The man was gone, and Luc didn't intend to lose her again as well. In a few seconds she would have fish scent frozen to her skin and clothes, yet she managed a wry smile and shrug when he gave her a stern look.

Luc pulled several coins from his pocket and gave them to the fishmonger. "Sorry for the inconvenience. I believe that should cover it."

"Aye, sir. That puts it 'bout right. An' she's welcome to shop 'ere anytime." He gave Avery a leery glance. "Long as she's with you, sir. Happy Christmas to you."

"Happy Christmas." Luc waved to him and the others still watching Avery shake out her skirts. Someone handed her what remained of her roasted nuts, and she thanked him while offering him a taste. He declined, so she stuck them in her cloak, only to realize it was a bit damp—and fishy. She pulled out a squirming surprise.

"Sorry, little friend. No room at the inn." Avery dropped the fish back in the upright barrel and carefully stepped away until her feet were on a safe surface—something not easy with slushy cobblestones everywhere.

Luc took her arm. "If I may," he asked. "I don't want you breaking any bones before the ball tonight. I need at least one other partner besides your mother."

She smiled brilliantly, unaffected by her escapade. "I shall be happy to dance with you, Luc. After I bathe for several hours, of course."

He wrinkled his nose and nodded in agreement. "I appreciate that consideration. I promise to do the same."

A breeze came off the water, and Avery closed her eyes against the cold, shivering violently against him. Good lord. Her entire bottom half was damp and it was a good twenty-minute walk in the snow to reach her home. Her beautiful pink lips were fading to blue. He leaned down and kissed them. Yes, icy. Gently he tasted the bottom and top providing heat with his lips, before breathing warm breath over them. He didn't care who saw. When he lifted his head, it seemed to have helped.

She smiled blissfully and Luc worried. She was entirely too sedate. Perhaps a reaction to the cold?

He took off her wet cloak and replaced it with his. "Can you make it?"

"That helps." She snuggled the cloak tighter and smiled up at him, still shaking. "Thank you."

He took off his gloves and put them in his cloak, then took off her wet gloves and did the same. "Give me your hands." She offered them up and Luc enfolded them in his, rubbing to get blood flow, then bending over to breathe more warming air into the tent his hands made around hers. Her rubbed some more.

"Better?"

She nodded. "That's the nicest thing anyone's ever done for me."

He laughed. "You look so pathetic, I almost believe you." He tucked her left arm under her right armpit, then pulled his cloak together so she could hold it with her free hand. Wrapping an arm securely around her shoulders, he led them up the gentle slope toward Greenwich Park.

"I think covering for you when you re-labeled all Cook's spices was nice."

"My mother was livid with you for weeks." She shuddered again and he squeezed. "I didn't know spices were so expensive. That was really nice. My mother knew it was me. She kept saying how awful you were just to upset me."

"But you never confessed."

"Of course not!" She smirked. "Then you would have looked like a liar. I couldn't have that on top of all your sins. I was preserving your honor."

"Inordinately kind of you."

"It was."

Luc was relieved she talked. The cold had not overcome her. They walked a little farther in silence before he asked the question on his mind. "Why didn't you have me come with you?"

"Then I would need a chaperone."

"You need one regardless."

"I know." She said it so wretchedly he could not push the point. "Sometimes I just like to walk alone. And breathe"—she huffed as the slope got steeper by the park—"and look at the world and the people in it without feeling so confined." She glanced up for his reaction. "Sometimes I like to do that."

He caught her eyes, still walking. "I understand."

Avery stared at him a moment. It had been a long time since anyone understood her. Luc always had. And he really seemed to now. She breathed a sigh of comfort and relief that she did not have to explain everything.

They continued to walk in silence, Avery intensely grateful to have Luc's heat to burrow into. She'd never been so desperately cold. If not for him, she would be miserable too, but he took care of her. She smiled despite her suffering. She felt wonderful inside. His concern and efforts to warm her body did magical things to her heart. She wanted to tell him then and there how much she loved him, and how she wanted to take care of him too...if only he would let her.

Luc finally broke the silence. "I thought perhaps you didn't trust me. You went to the magistrate. Did you find anything useful?"

"You followed me?"

"Only when I realized you were being followed." He took a breath, "But, yes, I would have followed you regardless. I thought we made a good team."

"We did." When he looked disappointed, she corrected herself. "We still do." That earned an appreciative smile. They walked several more steps. "Everything is more fun when I'm with you."

He nodded. "I think so too."

"You do?"

"Yes. I missed that most when I was gone."

"Then why didn't you come back sooner?" The question came out before she could stop herself. It had been on her mind every day he continued to seek her out and woo back her friendship. She didn't need the wooing; she needed to understand. But…wooing did warm her heart and make her feel special. *And loved.*

"It's like Rufus said."

"What did Rufus say?" Dear old Rufus was going to get thoroughly interrogated in exactly six minutes.

"Oh. That's right. You weren't there." He growled into her hair playfully. "That was just before I was sent to ravish you."

"My mother didn't send you to *ravish* me."

"I'm certain she was *hoping* I would."

She elbowed him gently. "You digress. What did Rufus say?"

"Ah. Yes."

Luc was silent, and Avery thought he debated sharing with her. Avery waited. She sensed whatever it was she could not force it from him. There were so many things he didn't tell her in the past that she didn't want to risk him drawing away again. She counted the seconds, a sense of importance building. Her ten seconds of patience paid off.

"He explained to the womenfolk how a man has to learn what he's made of. See who he is."

Not at all what she was expecting. Was he referring to himself? Luc had always been confident and known who he was. How could he not know what he was made of, how wonderful he was, how strong and good he was?

Hesitant to even suggest it, Avery spoke softly, looking ahead, as if the question and answer were not so important. "Is that what you were doing?"

She felt rather than saw him glance at her to judge her

reaction to the conversation.

"Well…yes. That, and I couldn't depend on my father's baronetcy to provide."

Avery kept her eyes forward, her voice casual. "Oh. I didn't know that."

"It's not something a man likes to discuss."

Avery stopped. Stunned. Until he had left Greenwich the first time, there had never been anything they could not tell each other. Or so she thought. "You could have. With me." How could he not know that?

He laughed at her suggestion, and she froze in place, her stomach turning with unease. What did that mean? Didn't he trust her?

"You're the last one I could have discussed it with."

Her eyes blinked with shock. "But…that makes no sense!" She turned home, to mask the sting of tears.

"Exactly." He dragged her along. "Avery, a man doesn't want the girl he cares about helping him become a man."

Avery was so upset, she almost missed the 'caring' part. Recovering her wits, she countered, albeit more emotionally than she intended. "But…that's so ungrateful! We were best friends. I would have done anything for you!"

"I didn't want you to."

"But, but…ohh." She trudged faster, confounded. Men were confused, emotional beings who'd rather destroy a woman's heart than ask for her help. Two more minutes and Rufus would get the lecture of his damn life. What was wrong with them?

"I've been studying sheep breeding. I think there's an opportunity to breed heartier sheep that can supply more wool."

Curious. She peeked at him then back to the road. What did one do with that information? "You were always very good at biology and the sciences. Your mother told me you've doubled your stock, and you harvested the fields early this year before the sudden weather that hurt so many. She's very proud of you. Many wished they had followed suit."

"It put us in a better position."

"To get another ram to mate?" she asked.

"Yes, but there's something else I need to tell you, before you go inside,

I—"

Anticipation and dread competed for her thoughts. They'd reached the side entrance to her home. Avery stepped onto the doorstep, so that they were nearly face to face. He seemed neither winded nor chilled.

"There's a position at the Naval Office in London."

*Oh please.* Her heart flipped with hope. Was he going to stay? The thought of having him home, seeing him regularly… *Please say you want the position. Please.*

"That would be wonderful. Your mother would be so happy."

He took her chin between his thumb and forefinger and lifted. "The thing is, London is a terrible place to view the stars."

Her stomach dropped. The side door to the kitchen opened.

"Miss Hilfington?" Mary took one breath and shrieked with horror. "Gads, Miss Avery. What happened? Ew. You stink and you're wet, and if you die on Christmas, twill be a very bad wedding omen for me." She shook her head at Luc and shooed him away. "Off you go. A'fore someone sees you besides meself."

"Just one more minute, Mary." Avery said. Luc had been about to tell her something important. She was certain.

"That's all it takes to catch a chill!"

"She's right. You need to get inside. We'll have time later." He leaned down and pecked Avery on the forehead. "You're still the most beautiful woman I've ever seen, even if you do smell like a fishmonger."

"Thank you. And thank you for taking care of me." She handed him back his cloak.

Mary shrieked when she saw Avery's wet and frozen skirts. "Miss Avery. Now!" She ran inside and ordered hot water for a bath.

Avery heard Cook and Campbell jump up concerned. She turned back to Luc.

"At least I am leaving you in good hands." Luc took her hands and gently kissed the top of each. "I shall look forward to tonight more than any night I have in a long while."

Avery brightened. "Me as well."

Suddenly she was filled with excitement, eager to make herself beautiful for him. It was going to be a wonderful night!

Mary literally yanked her inside. Luc lifted a hand in farewell, and the welcoming warmth of the kitchen nearly did her in.

"Ohhhh. Thank goodness. I'm freezing."

Mary, Cook and Campbell wrinkled their noses and gaped at her in horror.

"Yes, I know! I'll catch pneumonia, I stink like a fishmonger, and I'll need two baths before I smell human again. Please help me! I've not much time to recover before tonight!"

She wanted to look so stunning he would never think to leave her again. He wanted to speak to her about something. Did he wish to mend their relationship? His actions the last several days pointed toward that.

She spun on one foot and twirled out the door with a

final order.

"And send Rufus to me immediately!"

# CHAPTER TEN

Avery checked her timepiece—for the fifth time in two minutes. She paced by the fireplace, tapped fingers on the mantel, and confirmed the weather would allow the Rees's carriage through. Luc and his family were coming in for a Christmas toast, and then they would all travel together to the Astin ball.

Luc's carriage was large, though she hoped she would be squeezed next him for the short journey through the park to the Astins' magnificent castle-like home. Avery sniffed her hands again and finally relaxed. She'd slept in her second bath, soaking in lemon-scented water after using nearly all her precious perfumed soap, and emerged wrinkled but triumphant. Definitely no fishy odor left.

Getting useful information out of Rufus afterward had been another matter altogether. All he could explain was that men had to make something of themselves on their own—*at least the good ones did*. Avery thought there must be other pressures involved, but Rufus was virtually an esteemed elder of her family, so she dared not contradict him.

She verified the time again. Despite her excitement,

napping for two hours had not been an issue. Only now, energy and impatience coursed through her.

The rustle of silk outside the receiving room filled her with relief. Avery couldn't keep her own company much longer, and tonight had a rare eagerness for her mother's counsel and approval of her attire. If something was amiss, there was perhaps still time to change.

Clad in lavender ice, her mother entered with grace and elegance Avery hoped she could imitate. Her mother's expression dashed her hopes in an instant.

"Avery." She blinked—in either bewilderment or shock.

Avery held her breath, trying to read her mother's expression. "Is it my hair?" Mary had piled it high into a mass of stylish curls with just one long curl left hanging past her left temple, "to lure and beckon." She secretly hoped it would drive Luc insane, maybe enough for him to steal a kiss. However, by the look on her mother's face, she had perhaps missed the mark.

Her mother shook her head and suddenly pricks of tears appeared in her eyes.

"Mother!" Avery rushed to her, clasping her hands. "What is it? I thought you agreed the red dress would do. I—"

Her mother shook her head. Then smiled. Avery breathed with some relief.

"My darling," her mother began. "You look radiant." She squeezed Avery's hands. "You're in love, aren't you?" It wasn't a question.

Avery pulled away. "Oh, Mother." What could she say? She shrugged and admitted with a laugh. "Yes. I have loved Luc, forever. And now…I think he might love me too."

"Of course he does!"

Her mother's reassurance gave her a measure of confidence.

"He said there was a position open at the Naval Office. I think he might stay." Avery put a hand on her stomach, to breathe. "He wants to talk to me further."

Her mother squeezed her arms. "To propose marriage, no doubt!"

Avery hesitated. Was that what he meant? "I don't know. I just know he cares for me and I for him. I've missed him…so much."

"I know," her mother said, understanding. "Oh, my dear. I know. I'm so happy for you."

Rufus interrupted them. "Ma'am, your guests have arrived."

"Wonderful. Do bring them in."

Avery and Mrs. Hilfington stood waiting, and slowly but surely the uneven steps of her friend Ned sounded until he entered—alone.

"Yes, I know! I beat them to you," he said, leaning on a cane, and grinning merrily. "A very Merry Christmas!"

"Oh, Ned! You look dashing!"

Her mother agreed.

"My only regret is that I won't be able to dance with the two loveliest women in all of Greenwich. Make that three. Though Lady Rees has not danced in some time either. Rees and the Commodore are helping her up the steps. They sent me as the advance party."

"Being with friends has made all the difference in your temper. I think you are getting spoiled by Lady Rees."

Ned agreed. "She is most generous-hearted and loving, but I have other news."

Avery waited, interested and hopeful. "What is it?"

"I've accepted a position at the Naval Office in London. They don't seem to mind my current state and feel I will be an asset to their work."

Two mouths dropped. Had it not been in shocked

worry, Avery would have found it comical. Instead, her heart began to pound with in trepidation.

"That's wonderful!" the women said in unison, recovering in an instant.

Avery hurried forward to squeeze his hand in happiness. "Oh, Ned. Congratulations, I'm so pleased for you. And you will be reasonably close. You must promise not to stay away."

"Of course not. I'll need to get settled a bit, but Commodore Rees has given me several letters of introduction. It is a relief, I admit, to not worry about being useful."

"You would never have that worry, Ned," Avery insisted.

He shrugged.

"Are there additional positions? Perhaps you and Lieutenant Rees can work together?" Avery heard the concern mixed with curiosity in her mother's question.

"Even better news, has he not told you yet?"

Avery's foreboding spiked. Her mother shook her head.

"He's been offered Master and Commander—of any ship of his choice! Within reason of course, but it is a tremendous compliment to his skills as a leader and navigator. He's no doubt being modest on my behalf, so I am happy to share the good news."

The world tilted precariously and Avery put a hand on the nearest table, a stunned and quivery smile pasted to her face.

"Goodness. Blessings abound," her mother said.

Avery sensed her mother's quick glance, but they both remained cheerful and merry. Ned in his happiness did not seem to notice anything amiss.

"I will prepare our toasts," Avery said, seeking the opportunity to turn away from the others. She needed a moment. The champagne was chilling, but she did not trust herself to lift the bottle. She could not see clearly. Her vision telescoped to darkness, loneliness its mark.

The conversations she'd had with Luc this last week and today came rushing at her in a jumble, suddenly making sense. This was what he wanted to tell her. He needed the income. Perhaps he did not want to leave but had to? He might be gone two years at time, and very far from home. He could be shipwrecked, or lost. The odds went up terribly with those assignments. What if he didn't return? Her longitude watch would not be ready in time. She did not even know of anyone who might be close to a solution. If there was, she must find them. She could live as long as he was alive. It would be possible. They would be apart, but perhaps this time he would write. It was better than nothing. Better than not knowing anything.

She squeezed her eyes shut and opened them again, trying to focus. She heard the footsteps of the other guests. There was no time to prepare. She sensed him getting closer. She had to face him, greet him. She could not dwell on feelings now. She must get through the evening. And most of all, she must support Luc. That was the one thing he'd wanted from her. She understood now.

When she turned, her mother was beside her. Avery felt the quick, comforting squeeze of her hand. It helped. She was not entirely alone. She must remember that. She had family and dear friends.

She returned a tremulous smile, squeezed back to confirm she was well, then gave what she prayed was the most brilliant and joyous greeting one would give dear friends on a festive Christmas Eve.

Luc walked into to the room with his mother and uncle, in time to see Avery turn to her mother then to him. In an instant his entire world focused, centered, and zoomed in on the one thing he wanted—her.

She looked more stunning than ever in a luxurious red dress that was both elegant and alluring. Her glowing white skin and the exposed curve of her breast made him wonder why she ever bothered with clothes—other than the temperature of course. He shook his head. She should never wear clothes. He followed the graceful line of her neck, leading to an aristocratic chin and full red lips that should only be doing one thing—kissing him. Her rich, dark hair piled high tempted him beyond all that was civilized. He wanted to pull it part, rake his fingers through it, destroy the image of perfection she presented and release the passionate woman he knew was underneath. Beautiful was too inadequate a term to describe her.

All of her character, integrity, and humor seemed to radiate out of her body, and what a body! He swallowed, his mouth going dry.

Then she smiled a welcome that nearly knocked him backward. Their eyes met for the briefest of moments, hers dewy soft, unsettling him before she turned to his mother and uncle. Her attention to his family gave him a chance to stare unabashedly while his gut recovered. The rest of his manhood wouldn't be as easily controlled. A powerful desire possessed him, made him want to embrace her, and whisk her away. He could not imagine ever wanting otherwise.

It took another moment to understand his unsettled feeling. Something was wrong. He tried to meet her eyes to see what it was, to let her know he was here to help. Only she wouldn't look at him. Concerned, he stepped forward. He must have a moment with her, to touch her and comfort her.

Upon his approach she reached for two champagne glasses and held them out as if for self-protection. She beckoned his uncle. "Commodore Rees, will you do the honors. We have much to celebrate! Ned's new assignment and Luc's new commission. Congratulations!"

Luc stopped in his tracks. She'd heard. But he'd not yet told the Naval Office his decision. She smiled at him. Warmly. Genuinely. Perhaps he'd read her wrong. A champagne bottle popped and Avery had her mother hand out the glasses. She wanted to avoid him. He wouldn't have it. He took a glass from her, their hands touching, hers pulling away—part repelled, yet part drawn to him. He couldn't be mistaken about that.

Finally she met his eyes again, her glass lifted. "It's absolutely brilliant!"

Her mother embraced Luc. "We couldn't be more thrilled for you both. What grand adventures you'll have!"

"Indeed." What else could one say.

"Luc?" His mother spoke softly, beckoning him. He brought her a glass of champagne and leaned over. "You did not tell me you had accepted. Is this what you want?"

"I'm—" Before he could discuss it with his mother, Avery interrupted with enthusiasm.

"And the good news is that when my longitude watch is once again in working order you can take it with you for sea trials. Its accuracy can only be validated on one of the king's ships and there's no one I would trust more than you."

She meant it genuinely. Luc could see that. Damned it if didn't hurt. She would not miss him so much, and how useful he could be to her.

"This seems an appropriate time to let you all know that Avery has released me from our long-standing betrothal—and by long-standing I mean since birth." He walked toward her. "And I have accepted her decision. We remain friends." He reached out his hand, and she took it.

"Dear friends," she corrected. Then, as if on impulse, she leaned up and pecked his cheek, confirming her sisterly affection.

"Well!" All eyes turned to Mrs. Hilfington. "This is turning into an abysmal holiday."

The group laughed, and Commodore Rees patted her mother's shoulder with humor. It had never been a secret that she advocated the betrothal.

"Come sit with me, Constance," his mother said. "We can comfort each other."

The group gathered for a while, catching up on news, mostly Ned's new position since Avery was so interested, and soon it was time for them to continue to the ball. Luc craved the opportunity to speak with her alone, even if it was only the ballroom floor.

"Avery," her mother called to her. "I'm going to change my jewels before we leave. Will you assist me? This clasp is scratching me terribly."

Avery nodded and followed her mother.

"We'll be just a moment," Avery said. "I promise!"

Avery turned from the group, relieved to finally be able to relax her face. She followed her mother, her legs feeling as heavy as her spirit. At the top of the stairs, her mother pulled her into her chamber and shut the door.

"I cannot believe it!" She went to her dressing table and nearly yanked the pearl necklace from her throat, her eyes connecting with Avery's in her mirror. "How can he leave? And after leading you on so completely!"

"Mother," Avery sat on the bed and released a sigh, her throat choking up. "It is perhaps—" her voice croaked, and she cleared it. "Perhaps not what I thought."

"Do you have an understanding?"

Avery shook her head.

"I saw you both this afternoon. That was not the kiss of

man uninterested. Why, he sprinted to find you when I sent him."

"You saw us?"

"Of course. I could not help it. You didn't hear me the first time. Then I was so joyous that I snuck backward like a spy. Harry would have been proud. I had to sneeze four times before you actually heard me."

Avery gave a little laugh. Her mother lifted a jade necklace for approval and she shook her head. "The opal necklace, perhaps."

"Hmmph. I don't think I'll wear anything. I'm too upset and I don't feel merry in the least."

"Nor I, Mother."

Mrs. Hilfington turned in her chair. "I cannot believe Luc took advantage of you. I had not thought that of him."

Avery stood, her mother joining her. "He must go. He has a property to maintain, and barely any funds with which to do it. And men cannot be beholden to others in that way."

"Plenty of them are!"

"But not the good ones. I think too, that Luc wants to explore the world and see what he is made of…and what he can make for himself. And he needs to be able to take care of his responsibilities. I do not blame him for not wanting to take another responsibility. My dowry, if we dare call it that, would hardly put a dent in his monthly expenses. It is simply not to be, at least for now. We must support him and be encouraging."

"Blast him!"

Avery laughed. Her mother embraced her and for a change Avery held her tight.

"I love you, Avery. I could not have asked for a more wonderful woman to be my daughter. You make me more proud every day. It is my only sin."

Avery squeezed her mother's hands and released her. She had several hours that she must survive before she could curl up in bed. She must think of other things. Useful things. Like how her solution for longitude would work and would assure Luc's safety and many others. She must stay positive. If not, she would surely crumble before the eyes of the man she loved and her pride would not let her accept his pity. That would ruin every memory she had.

And it seemed memories were all that she would have.

# CHAPTER ELEVEN

They were dancing.

For a short period of time Avery could pretend she wouldn't miss him. Only Avery had stopped pretending the first time Luc had left…well, actually the second. She hung on for nine months pretending there had been some misunderstanding, or a horrible incident that had taken Luc away in the night. When he came home and left again without seeing her, she'd been crushed. She never told anyone, but her heart had ached for two years, and her tears every night had been muffled by her feather pillow. Worst of all, she had stopped pretending, which made it very hard not to cry.

"You look magnificent, Avery."

"Thank you."

The music swelled and they released hands to make a turn before returning to face each other. He bowed, she curtsied and they linked hands again.

"I'd hoped to talk to you further before anyone found out about the offer."

She nodded, gazing politely past his shoulder, and attempting a smile. It didn't work. She was angry. As much as she thought she understood, and tried to understand, somewhere between the cramped quarters of the carriage, and the crush of the ballroom, she discovered that she hated Luc. He was selfish and unkind and had led her to believe he cared for her.

"It was too generous for me to simply turn it down."

"Of course. You have responsibilities. I understand. You owe me nothing. We are not betrothed." She added, "And even when we were, you did not feel obligated to explain, so nothing has changed. Your life is your own." It sounded bitter when said aloud. Not what she intended despite being angry. It was Christmas, after all. She should not take her hurt feelings out on him, even if he did nearly ravish her this afternoon, pretending to care when he knew he would not be staying. She took a calming breath before smiling gaily. "And the sea is a much better place to stargaze," she noted, reminding him of their earlier conversation.

"You're angry."

"I'm resigned to being a woman."

"You make a wonderful woman."

She snorted. *Not wonderful enough for you it seems.* Damnation, if this conversation continued, she might lose the tenuous control she held on the floodgates of passion and fury burning to spew forth and expose her for a less then genteel woman.

"There isn't a woman I admire more in the world."

Excellent. Leave it to Luc to diffuse wrath.

"Thank you," she said flatly. Did he think that would warm her heart during the long lonely nights he was away?

"Avery, I would like to speak with you privately. About the commission. Will you meet me on the west balcony?"

"Indeed not. We have just escaped a forced betrothal. You think to destroy our lives again?"

"Destroy?"

"That is exactly what it did. I have no desire to go back to that sad state of affairs. Besides, my next set is with Professor Halley. I wouldn't miss that for the world." She added, "He admires me as well."

His blue eyes stared at her, hot and irritated—or frustrated—she could not tell. Either way, it was only what he deserved. They finished with a bow and curtsey, and he escorted her to the side. She had not meant to irritate him, but he should not expect her to be blindly adoring any longer. Thinking of her behavior in her bedroom this afternoon made her flush again with humiliation. He was leaving and she must move on with her life. She would do that.

"Merry Christmas, Mrs. Halley. Professor Halley." Avery gave the couple a cheery greeting, desperate for distraction. "Was that Sir Isaac with you? That's a rare treat."

"Indeed! I had to drag him out," Halley said. "His niece and her husband brought him."

"His home was the target of a theft," Mrs. Halley shared.

"What!" Avery halted, immobilized. She thought of the list in her box at home. "Did they take an orrery, perhaps?"

Halley and his wife gasped. "How did you know?"

Luc stood at attention.

"I believe the same scoundrels who stole my timepiece have stolen many other devices and papers, most of which purport or contribute to a solution for longitude."

"It seems to be a ring of desperate lunatics," Luc said. "I'm not sure yet if they are dangerous or just foolish."

"I shouldn't like to find out," Mrs. Halley said.

The music started, and Professor Halley led her to the dance floor. "Am I mistaken or is there tension between you and your young man?"

"He is not mine, Professor. He belongs to the king's

navy. Greenwich is simply a port for his amusement."

"Indeed," Halley frowned.

"Indeed," Avery confirmed. "He will be leaving soon. He has been offered Master and Commander."

"Indeed! Well, that is a high compliment. You must be very proud of him."

Avery didn't know what to say. Only another man would think she should be proud of him.

"He is not mine to be proud of, but it is an accomplishment he can add to his list. He is very versatile. He's breeding sheep on his property, you know."

"Yes, we spoke of it. I've recommended some people for him to engage. I thought he would be here to do it, though."

"He has a competent steward."

"And you, my dear? It is Christmas, you are surrounded by many who love you, you look simply majestic…"

"Thank you."

"And yet you are not happy."

"I am content."

"Resigned."

"It is the same."

"For one who values precision, I know you don't believe that," Halley said.

She changed the subject. "Were there any clues as to who might have stolen the orrery from Sir Isaac?"

"Not a one, but you seem to be on to something."

"Maybe. I fell upon a list," she confessed.

"I'm listening."

"Then I stole it."

Halley laughed merrily earning some glances.

"From Dr. Llewellyn. He might be the ringleader, after all."

"Never would have pinned him for that sort."

"His brother died at sea."

"No excuse."

"Maybe." Avery had begun to think love made one behave irrationally. Dangerously even. "You're the only on the list who has not been robbed."

"I'm on the list! Flattering, to be sure."

"You should be careful, Professor Halley."

"Ach. I never leave home. Do you think they would break in while I'm there?"

Avery froze on the dance floor. "Is anyone there now?"

Halley stopped as well. "No. Georges is here. He drove the carriage. The others are day employees and with their families until tomorrow. You think someone has been watching me?"

Avery didn't answer but hurried off the dance floor, Halley in tow. They passed Luc, who asked what had happened.

"Your star map, Professor. Is it locked up? It was on the list," Avery said.

"Nothing's locked up," Halley blurted, his expression astonished.

"What list?" Luc asked. He followed behind Avery as the two weaved between revelers.

Halley gave a furtive look over his shoulder. "The one she stole from Llewellyn."

"When?"

"At his sister-in-law's home."

"Avery!"

"I know! Don't criticize."

"I'm not. You think the observatory will be robbed? Tonight?"

"It seems possible," Avery said. "Professor Halley was the only one on the list left to steal from. What better time than when we are all preoccupied. It's not as if he is gone very often."

"True enough," Halley quipped. "Dedicated to science, these days."

Avery grunted with humor at him. "And to wine."

"Of course. Where's the fun otherwise, my dear."

The two men followed Avery as she hurried out the ballroom near the manor's grand entrance. Luc went right, Halley went left, and Avery rushed forward. She stood outside on the front viewing deck. Carriages crowded the street, providing little chance of a quick escape.

Shivering at a blast of wind, she turned toward the observatory and stared. The silhouetted building could barely be made out in the dark. She shivered again and covered her chest uselessly with her gloved hand as icy air wound down through her bodice. Just then, hands and heat surrounded her shoulders from behind as Luc wrapped her cloak around her, and tossed another to Halley who joined them.

"I let my wife know I might be stepping out for a bit," Halley said.

Avery continued to stare at Flamsteed House, wishing for stars or moon to provide light, but the sky remained dark, blocked by the promise of more snow. The men joined her on either side, looking up at the hill as well.

"Should we go investigate?" Halley asked.

"I don't know," Avery said. "I could be a lunatic like Luc says. I'd hate to pull you from the loveliest ball of the—"

Avery stopped. A flash of light moved inside the observatory illuminating for only an instance through a window on the north side.

"Why!" Halley gasped.

"Did you see that?" Avery asked.

"You were not expecting anyone, I presume?" Luc asked.

"No! And Georges is with us. No doubt warming his feet in a kitchen somewhere."

"I'm here, sir," Georges said behind them.

The three jumped in surprise. Halley slapped him on the shoulder. "Excellent timing. We're being robbed. Where's the carriage?"

Georges didn't question, though the news did seem to give him pause. "We are parked there," he pointed. The carriage rested directly in front of them, trapped and surrounded by a hundred others.

"Good lord, man. What were you thinking?"

"That you like to enjoy a good celebration and this was the best location to assist you home, sir."

"Indeed." Halley laughed. "Very well."

"This way," Luc said, already on the move. "My carriage is better situated." Luc assisted Avery as the four hurried through slushy snow, their breath making white puffs of air before them. Luc directed a number of grooms to move, his own man, alert and ready. Luc sent him to the back of the carriage while Avery hauled herself to the reins.

"Avery, no!"

"Just get up here and hurry!" she said.

"Get in!" Luc told Halley and Georges. The two men scrambled inside while Luc climbed next to Avery, the carriage already in motion.

She guided them toward observatory. The path up the snowy hill was treacherous in a carriage—even at a slower pace—and added to her anxiety as wheels slipped and horses whinnied.

Avery exhaled with relief when they made it to a level and safe area. As her eyes adjusted and Halley's home came into view, she spotted two horses on the path across the front of the house. They were not hidden, but then the thieves clearly did not expect company. Georges and Luc bounded from the carriage and rushed to the house. Avery climbed down at the same time as Halley, and tried to think how the villains had entered, for it appeared Georges had locked the front entrance.

She tugged her cloak more tightly about her throat and launched toward the front part of the park, checking windows methodically. Likely the thieves had found an open door in the back, but just in case...

There was a light thud in the dark before something pulled Avery from behind. A man. And his arm proceeded to tighten around her neck. She clutched the stranger in panic, squeaking. The sound died as the hold increased, and the black night became even darker.

Luc followed Georges and the two men rushed to the study where Halley kept his maps and other documents.

Halley joined them seconds later, out of breath but quickly making a survey of the contents.

"Damnation! The bloody bastards. My star maps, my notes on magnetism—they're gone! They dare rob the Royal Observatory! I'll have their heads, I will."

Luc lifted a hand to silence him. Fortunately the men obeyed. There was a sound from not far away. They rushed to next room in time to see a man bursting through glass to escape, a satchel over his shoulder.

Luc turned to follow then realized something more important. "Where's Avery?"

Halley froze. "She was outside. Checking..." He looked at the window meaningfully. Luc bolted.

Outside the front door Luc began to shout, a heavy sense of dread burning his stomach with every call she didn't answer. He ran toward where the villain escaped and saw two horses stealthily departing the grounds.

"Avery! Avery!" In his search he nearly tripped over her. A flash from a lantern behind him revealed blood-red snow. Horror and shock filled his soul as he fell to the ground only to realize the red was her dress. She stirred as he lifted her in his arms, slowly coming to while he ran his hands over her body searching for injury.

A delicate touch found his hand and pushed it away. "Do not take liberties with me, you scoundrel."

"Avery! You were in a dead faint." Relief coursed through him. "Are you injured?"

More awake, she began to stand, remembering what had happened. "I'm fine. He choked me!" She patted down her body." I'm fine. What are you waiting for? They're escaping!"

She hurried forward but swayed. Luc steadied her, despite a stubborn, dismissing shove. Again, she climbed up front.

"I'll drive this time."

"The hell you will."

He grasped the reins from her weak grip. "I draw the line at some things, dear friend. Hang on." He yelled similar orders to the men in the carriage.

The path down was much faster than up, and the horses, free to lead, kicked up snow, sending a rush of cool air and ice in their faces.

"There's a gun in the box below the seat. Can you reach it?" Luc shouted, his grip and gaze concentrated on getting down the steep road in one piece.

Avery bent, her dress clearly not enabling the simple maneuver. He clasped her around the waist as she twisted, to assure she didn't fall off the carriage altogether as they bounced left to right with increasing force.

She reached the gun, but couldn't get the shot. She

hoped the threat of a pistol would do the job…or not be needed.

They reached the bottom of the hill, and he heard Avery's relief before she pointed left.

"That way!"

On even ground, they raced forward, not anticipating the coming turn. The villains went right. The carriage could not—at least not without tipping.

"Take the next turn!" Avery directed.

He did. The carriage barely fit but at least the road was clear…or so he thought. It was hard to tell in the dim light.

They sped recklessly to the next corner, making good time—until their carriage hit a patch of packed snow that sent them flying.

"Whoaaa!"

Luc's body lifted off the seat and he reach instinctively for Avery.

They landed in an awkward heap, miraculously back in the seat, with him mostly lying on Avery's lap. She pushed him up, though maintained a tight clutch on his arm. After a split second of silence they looked at each other and laughed—a nervous, crazy laughter that they were still alive.

Luc spurred the horses on, cornering to the right, and caught sight of his prey cornering left toward them.

He charged.

"Luc! We'll crash," Avery warned, as horses continued toward collision. Miraculously all turned down the main road at once without disaster, their quarry now racing parallel, nearly close enough to touch.

Luc handed Avery the reins, and stepped over her lap to the other side of the carriage.

An instant later, he jumped.

He heard Avery's frantic scream as he toppled a villain from his horse and they both landed hard in the packed snow. This one had the maps. Luc dealt a crushing blow that helped release most of his fury. He dragged the wobbling man to his feet and relieved him of his plunder. He would have followed up with another strike had he not needed information—such as where they were headed.

He looked down the road. Avery continued to chase the other villain with only an empty weapon and two old men for protection. Perhaps jumping was not his smartest decision.

He grabbed the man by the scruff of his neck and pulled him along. If something happened to Avery, he'd never forgive himself.

# CHAPTER TWELVE

The horseman took a sharp corner and Avery dropped the pistol, clinging to the reins that ripped through her thin gloves and tore at her palms. Ignoring the burning sensation, she stood, her knees bent for balance, and concentrated on the next turn, praying the carriage did not tip.

It did.

She leaned nearly sideways toward the suspended wheels, hoping for the slightest weight to bring the carriage back to earth.

It worked.

Relieved, she pulled the reins, slowing the carriage as she spotted the man abandoning his horse and escaping into a two-story storefront connected on both sides by shops. She realized she was back at the watch shop by the stables.

Confident of knowing where she was, Avery secured the pistol and hurried to the ground. With her tight gown and shaky nerves, her legs nearly collapsed in the snow. She caught herself, one hand maintaining her grip on the gun while the other grasped the carriage for support.

Luc's groom joined her at the front of the carriage, his

expression grim.

"If you don't mind, ma'am, I think I'm best qualified to be drivin' ya home."

"Agreed. Will you watch the carriage? We'll be just a moment."

She was joined by an equally shaken Halley and Georges. Halley's long white wig angled sideways, severely askew, while Georges appeared as if his hair had been styled to stand straight up.

"Where's Rees?" Halley asked.

She looked down the road. Empty. Luc could be dead, lying in the road with a broken neck.

Then again—a shadow came into view. Luc.

"He jumped. He'll catch up." She turned and tried the door of the clock shop.

"'He jumped'? 'He'll catch up'?" she heard Halley repeat, seeming dismayed.

Georges gently pushed her aside and kicked through the door. He reached in and turned the knob, before pushing it open for her.

"A man of many talents, I've always said." Halley straightened his wig and nodded to Georges.

Avery led with the pistol, following the urgent sound of voices.

"Hide everything! They're right behind me."

"You're right about that," Avery said. She aimed straight ahead, aware the excitement of the evening had made mush of her better judgment.

There were five of them.

Armed with a one-shot pistol, her spirit sank. She didn't even have one shot.

Avery recognized the man speaking. "Dr. Llewellyn."

"Miss Hilfington. I thought our paths might cross again."

Avery held the gun steady. The five men did not move. They seemed to be having a drink. No doubt toasting the table filled with longitude booty stolen from all around Greenwich and beyond.

"Your device was very clever," Llewellyn said. "You did one better than my brother. He would have been interested to meet you."

"And I him. His widow is very kind. You take advantage of her."

"I only seek to save lives. Same as you."

"We're not the same."

"Are we not?" he mocked. "I believe you took something of mine."

"I sought to end this thievery."

"The end justifies the means, then?"

She stood silent, caught by the truth. She'd stolen.

"Perhaps it was you who took advantage of a kindly widow," Llewellyn suggested.

"Enough wordplay, doctor."

Avery jumped at Luc's deep voice behind her, heavy with threat.

He handed the satchel of star maps to Halley. "The evidence speaks for itself." Llewellyn sat with his mute friends. "Alas, and none of it to any avail, for we have soundly disproved all solutions by methods of the stars and machines.

Avery's stomach flipped. "What do you mean?"

"Gravity, my dear," Llewellyn said. "Your clock, though a brilliant bit of horology, does not account for changes in the earth's gravitational pull. It will be deadly accurate on land, and perhaps for a time at sea, but you missed a vital calculation. I was somewhat disappointed myself."

Avery stared blankly, a calculation running in her head, turning the thought over in her mind, until it hit her. "Oh, no. The movement of the levers will be affected, similar to how a pendulum would." Her body went weak with dismay and somebody slid a chair beneath her.

She accepted, laying her gun on the table. "I'm an idiot." Nobody moved for a long while. She was grateful for the moment to gather herself. *Luc.* She lifted her head, heartbroken and defeated. He would be gone. His life left to chance, like all the others. The complete lack of control of his fate ripped through her insides, making her nauseous with fear and loss.

"What of the star maps? Why bother?" she asked, desperate.

"Aye, we thought to sell the bundle in a secret auction," one man confessed sounding depressed.

"Not very honorable, Llewellyn," Halley said.

The doctor shrugged. "Research costs money. The crown offers a prize with no resources to prove out a solution. And—" he said pointedly. "There's only one Astronomer Royal."

"Rightly so," Halley said, undisturbed by the man's tone.

Avery's thoughts continued to spin. "Have none of you even an inkling of a solution or method? You must have had some inspiration as you...*collected* all of this."

"I think you were the closest, Miss Hilfington," Llewellyn said, a hint of admiration in his voice.

"And yet it seems I am not close at all." She closed her eyes against the bitterness of loss that threatened to envelope her. Luc would leave without a hope of navigational certainty. Her studies had been an abysmal failure. She opened her eyes to find him watching her and gripped her stomach. The thought of losing him made her ill. She located the whisky bottle.

"May I have a drink?"

The men hurried to get her a clean glass. "Someone will

figure it out, miss. Probably not in our lifetime."

Halley, Georges, and Luc stood guard near Llewellyn ready to move should it be necessary. It began to seem less and less necessary.

These were not killers or criminals. They were not even very good thieves. Perhaps like Llewellyn, they were simply misguided.

Avery drank the whisky provided. It stung her throat and brought tears to her eyes, but she gave a weak thanks.

"You'll have to return everything," she told them.

They stared at her, Luc included.

"Ya mean, ya ain't going to tell the magistrate?" one of the men asked.

Avery looked at Halley.

He shrugged. "No harm done." He affixed his wig. "You gave us a good run though."

The men laughed. Luc shook his head. "I jumped from a racing carriage!"

The room went silent.

"Are you harmed?" Avery asked.

He lifted his coat to reveal a tear under the arm. "My Christmas coat is ruined."

Avery tilted her head. "But are you injured?"

"That's not the point." He folded his arms over his chest. No one spoke for a long moment, and then suddenly everyone in the room burst out laughing.

Georges was the first to break the barriers between the men. "I wouldn't mind a little drink m'self. It's bloomin' cold out."

Llewellyn supplied glasses while Halley fit right in pouring rounds. Luc made arrangements to return the stolen items.

Avery could not move. She could not celebrate. She could not even feel anything at the moment save something akin to abject despair. It sucked the very life from her.

When Luc offered his hand to leave, she simply stared.

"You're tired," he said.

She nodded. That was the only explanation for the hollow ache in her chest. She accepted his hand, and held it tightly in her own, allowing him to guide her to the carriage. She did not want to let him go. With one last squeeze on his fingers, she released, and settled herself in the carriage. Resigned.

Avery did not recall much of the ride home, or the conversation about the longitude ring, or even Luc's plans to drop her at home and fetch the rest of the family. It had begun to snow again. She gazed out the window, watching flakes fluttering by the carriage.

She wished the men Merry Christmas and Luc escorted her to her door.

"It's not done yet, Avery. Your sea watch may yet hold the solution," he said.

She nodded agreeably, for there was nothing left to say, and it was the polite thing to do when someone tried to comfort. He bent as if to kiss her forehead, but she pushed him away. With faithful timing, Rufus opened the door. Avery entered and walked straight to her room, leaving Luc to answer all the questions old Rufus spouted in worry.

Mary helped her out of her dress and she lay in bed under the covers, staring into the darkness. She was still awake when her mother checked on her, but pretended to sleep even when her mother sat on the mattress and brushed her cheek.

"Harry Rees kissed me tonight," her mother said.

Avery felt a shock go through her body, but said nothing. She didn't want to talk. Not tonight. She didn't have the energy.

"It was a long time coming," her mother added.

Avery remained silent, eyes closed, breathing in and out. Eventually her mother pecked her on the head like when she was a child.

"Merry Christmas, my dear daughter."

Avery listened to her mother's steps cross the floor. Avery knew about longing and loneliness. So did her mother. She did not wish anyone a lifetime of it. Before the door could close Avery sprang up in bed.

"You don't need my permission, Mother," she said quickly. "But he is a good man. I like him very much." She paused and her voice choked a little. "I'd like him even more if he made you happy."

"Thank you, Avery."

"Merry Christmas." Then she added the words she didn't say enough. "I love you."

"I love you too." Her mother's voice broke with emotion. "Sleep well."

Avery reclined again, huddling back under the covers.

The door closed softly behind her mother, and finally Avery pulled the feather pillow to her face, pressing it tight, to muffle the sobs that wrenched her body.

Sleep evaded her. Despite exhaustion and body aches from her adventures, her slumber was fitful. Her eyes ached, feeling itchy and dry when the morning arrived. The sun was not yet up, but Avery dressed in her warmest gown and stood by the window waiting for a hint of light that said it was safe to take a morning walk. It came slowly, revealing a winter wonderland with each ray that glistened on white. The pink sky would soon be blue.

A perfect Christmas day.

She reached for her timepiece, about to slip it over her

head. She stopped. Today she would stop worrying about time. It was time after all to accept her life. Counting minutes would not make the days any easier or more manageable.

Leaving the beloved watch on her vanity table, she put on heavy boots, gloves and a cloak, and hurried out the door to the snow-covered park. Walking in the cold was the one thing that always revived her, and sunrise on Greenwich would ease her soul. At least she prayed it would.

The observatory had a decorative coating of white, as did the surrounding trees. She made her way up the hill by habit, heading toward the observatory and the best view of London across the river. The exercise warmed her and Avery pushed her hood back, lifting her face to the morning sun, relishing the sting of cold air on her face after a night of hot tears.

She paused when another figure in black came into view, approaching her from the observatory. A man. His head down, hands in pockets.

He looked like Luc.

His head lifted. It was Luc.

Avery continued forward, compelled to be near him and talk to him alone, even for a few minutes. She didn't know when he would leave or when the opportunity would arise to speak again, but she had to be on good terms with him before he left. And he had to know he would always have a friend in her.

His pace quickened as well. He looked equally tired but smiled, and when he opened his arms to her, it was the most natural thing in the world to accept his embrace. She wrapped her arms under his heavy coat and rested her cheek on his chest.

"You're out alone again."

"Morning is peaceful. There's never anyone but me."

"Except today."

"Except today," she agreed, snuggling against his warmth. She felt his head rest on hers.

"I didn't know how to comfort you last night." He pulled her tighter. "I'm so sorry."

Fresh tears began to stream over her cheeks.

"I know when your father died, your world changed. I never meant to scoff at your efforts, I was worried about you. I didn't even consider that you might also need the prize money."

She rubbed her cheek in the cloak to wipe the tears before speaking. "Maybe Halley and his friends are right and the solution will come from the stars, not a timekeeper."

"You did brilliant work regardless."

She leaned back and sniffed. "Spoken like a true friend."

He brushed her cheeks with his thumbs, catching remnants of moisture. "Always, Avery. I will always be your friend. I only wish I could take away your pain."

Her eyes filled again and she turned away. "Oh, Luc." Avery shook her head. "I don't weep for what I've lost. I have cried those tears." She turned back trying to control the flood that threatened. "I weep for you!" she confessed. "I weep at the thought of you at sea, far away and possibly suffering the same fate as my father. *That* is what I cannot bear. I thought if I could keep you safe…if anyone could solve longitude and give you a chance to return home with some certainty, then I could manage it. I could live without you, but I cannot bear the thought of the world without you."

She rubbed her eyes. "Every time news arrives of a ship lost or a storm at sea, I would be ill wondering if you were safe. And it seemed all the worse that you left because of me. Because of that damned betrothal. I wanted you to be free so you would not have to leave, but it doesn't matter. I have no control over any of it. And I cannot bear it, Luc. I will not ask you to stay because of me. But you cannot stop my heart from aching because of it." She wiped the next wave of tears furiously.

Luc took her by the shoulders, blue eyes searching hers. "What are you saying? Avery? Tell me there is still a place for me in your heart."

She sniffled through her smile. "Of course, you idiot. I love you. That is the most constant thing in the world. More constant than gravity or magnetism or the stars. I've always loved you."

"I thought perhaps I'd pushed you too far. That we could not find our way back."

"You did push too far. You were awful, leaving how you did. I'll never forgive you."

"I left because of you."

"I didn't know what our parents had promised."

"No." He shook his head, his eyes gentle on her. "It wasn't that, Avery. It was because you were wonderful. Perfect. Confident. You knew who you were. And I…" He paused, and lifted her chin to face her directly. "I only knew who I was with you. I had to see what I was made of on my own. And I desperately wanted to be able to offer you more. I knew I couldn't do that if I stayed. But I also knew leaving you"—his voice grew thick with emotion—"leaving you would be the hardest thing I ever had to do. I could only do it once, Avery. That's why I avoided you. When I saw you last week at the hospital, I knew I would never leave again, even if my plans were not yet complete."

"What plans?" Avery asked meekly, afraid to hope.

"For the baronetcy. I've been studying and having the steward experiment, Avery. You might think being at sea is a grand adventure, but it's actually quite dull. After my first trip home I knew enough to try a breeding experiment. After my second we had a small flock of new lambs. The wool is thicker and grows longer. This year I had enough to buy the adjacent property. To diversify," he explained. "And we still made a profit, even with the expenses. I think it will continue."

"I'm sure it will, Luc."

"Enough for me to stay and run it myself." He searched her eyes. "It's not much yet, but it's a beginning. We could build it together. You always liked the property. It's the perfect place—

"—to view stars." She finished for him.

"I was hoping you'd think so."

"And I could work on my clock. I have an idea using only springs."

"You do?"

"Yes, it just occurred to me when I thought of how pretty the property is in the spring, and then—bing!" she said, excited.

He laughed. "You don't mind a simple life?"

Avery's heart pounded rapidly. "I only wanted you." She hesitated. "But what of Master and Commander? Do you really want to stay?"

"When I said it was too generous an offer to *simply* turn down, I meant that there were many men who thought well enough of me to make the recommendation. I could not say no without giving them an explanation in person. And no, the sea doesn't lure. It's much more fun having adventures with you."

"Why didn't you tell me?"

"Forgive me. Please." He took her hands, his eyes filled with emotion. "I was waiting until we could talk privately…and I could organize my thoughts and what I would say. But then you were so happy to have me test your sea watch." He put a hand over his heart. "I was crushed."

"I was trying to be supportive!" She laughed, tears coming again.

"Indeed."

"Indeed!" she insisted. "And it hurt terribly to take the high road."

His chest shook with humor. He pulled her in for a squeeze then cradled her head in his hands so she could see his smile. "Forgive me for leaving you, Avery. And forgive our parents for the betrothal. It terrified me to think of being married so soon—before I knew myself or tested myself in the world. I didn't want you to wake up one morning and find me lacking."

"Luc! I never thought that. You always challenged me and brought out the best in me."

"And you for me." He brushed a strand of hair behind her ear, a half grin teasing his lips. "You were always my true north. All roads lead to you."

Avery laughed, then sighed as cool lips came down on hers, and arms pulled her back into his embrace. Home.

"I love you, Avery. I hope you'll once again be my best friend."

He lifted his head for an answer. She nodded, unable to deny him.

"Yes."

"And soon, perhaps you will consent to be my wife?"

"Oh, Luc." Tears welled up again.

"Yes?"

She nodded vigorously. "Yes. Oh, yes!" She launched herself into his arms, taking his lips with passion.

A popping sound distracted them. They turned to find Halley on the path above in a heavy robe with Georges catching champagne in some glasses. "I recognized your magnetic connection from the beginning! Good news, my young friends?" he shouted.

"Indeed," Luc shouted back. "You've very keen observation, Professor."

"And an excellent telescope!" He lifted a glass. "Bring the dear girl and come celebrate. It's a merry Christmas at last!"

"We're coming!" Avery called up.

Halley planted the champagne and two glasses in the snow. "Collect it when you get here. I'm freezing Georges's arse off!" Georges waved then joined Halley inside.

Avery reached for her timepiece then remembered she'd left it at home.

"What is it, love?"

"My watch. I left it at home. I wanted to mark the time. The time when we started our lives together."

"There are other ways to mark time."

"Indeed?" She caught his cocky glance, suspicious of the sudden twinkle.

"Yes, indeed. Would you like to know my favorite?"

"I'm quite certain I would," she answered.

Luc pulled her into his arms and proceeded to mark their beginning with a kiss that made her see stars.

And Avery Hilfington, who'd spent years keeping time, finally lost all track of it.


# THE END

## ABOUT THE AUTHOR

There are few things more important in my writing career than telling a great story, a fun story, and sometimes one that inspires us to be a little better than we are. I hope in reading this story you gained comfort, laughs, or an escape from your every day life. Thank you for spending a little time with me and my "friends" who try to fill these pages with laughter and love.

Merry Christmas, and whatever holidays you celebrate, may you have Happy Holidays, every day.

**Trish Albright**

## A LITTLE BIT ABOUT LONGTITUDE

While you might be disappointed that our heroine Avery did not solve longitude, you might also be interested to learn that it was a self-educated man, of humble beginnings, who through his own inventiveness, passion, and determination, beat out the likes of Isaac Newton, Edmond Halley, and a slew of other renown thinkers, to single-handedly solve the problem of longitude.

John Harrison was born in 1693, in England, and spent the first part of his career as a carpenter. By 1730, when he had a possible mechanical solution to longitude, the Board of Longitude was nowhere to be found—they had never actually met, since no solutions had been worthy of review. Harrison went to the most famous of the board—Dr. Edmond Halley, at the Royal Observatory in Greenwich.

Halley was well liked, despite being denounced by Flamsteed, the former Royal Astronomer, for drinking brandy, swearing too much, and cavorting like a schoolboy.

Halley was interested, like most others of his time, in an astronomical solution, not a mechanical one. Still, having an open mind and impressed by Harrison, he became a supporter. It was nearly 20 years more of design, build, and sea trials before John Harrison was finally awarded the longitude prize in 1759 for his timekeeper, the H-4. His story is one of self-belief, ingenuity, learning, and tenacity.

To learn more about this fascinating piece of history, check out my favorite source, *The Illustrated Longitude* by Dava Sobel and William J.H. Andrewes.

**Excerpt From:**

**SIREN'S SONG**

CHAPTER ONE

*1787, Morocco*

Moments like this made her life legendary.

Being a practical sort, she preferred being a living legend.

An Arabian guard yanked her thick, long braid, demanding attention she refused to give. Undeterred, he hooked her bound arms, currently tied from behind, and dragged sideways towards the auction block. It was uncomfortable, not to mention, the height of rudeness.

Stumbling, but stubborn to the end, Alexandra Stafford levered bare feet against the hardwood steps and pressed backward against the guard with all her strength, her body nearly horizontal, stretched open to the crowd of attentive buyers.

Another figure sauntered into her peripheral vision and the face of her kidnapper appeared as he bent down, nonchalantly, to observe her distress. His hand lifted to halt the guard. Tilting his sun-darkened face parallel to hers, he frowned with a disingenuous expression of worry, shaking his head over her situation. The sour smell of tobacco emanated from his breath and skin, and Alex grimaced in disgust, before unleashing her fury.

"I swear if you do this, my family will hunt you down, cut you limb from limb, gut you like a pig, and feed you to the sharks, you miserable, sonofa—."

She cut off, choking, as Reginald Paxton blew smoke in her face. Her body convulsed with hacking coughs, and the guard took advantage to yank her back into standing position. Alex kicked out at Paxton with rage, her bare feet doing little damage to the parts she could reach. He laughed. It infuriated her further to think he was laughing at her puny efforts. Once freed, she would kill him. With any luck, a few different ways.

"Tell me where the map is, and I can make this all go away, Miss Stafford."

"I told you." The guard painfully tightened his grip on her. "I don't know anything—" She slammed her heel down on the guard's foot. "—About some stupid map."

The guard whacked her in the side of the head, causing her brain to rattle.

Alex faked a recovery she didn't feel, raised her head, and smiled.

Incensed, Paxton waved for the man to proceed.

"No! You bastard! I'm an American. I'm a free woman," Alex screamed, fighting violently as she was forced toward the platform. Her efforts were so fierce another guard came to assist.

"Someone help me!" she begged, searching desperately

for a sympathetic face or word from the crowd. There were none. Only the foreign sounds of Arabic. She understood enough to heighten her fear, as she was dragged onto the small stage and held in place.

In her short life she'd had many roles—daughter, heiress, sea captain, and now she thought bleakly, slave. Boston was a lifetime away and she was at the wrong end of a sale gone bad. Very bad. Fear no longer prickled the hairs at the back of her neck, but suffocated the life from her with dizzying force. She swore to kill Paxton for this—if her father didn't get to him first.

Forcing self-pity aside, she took stock of escape options. They appeared dismal at best.

To her left, the door she entered, was protected by a long hallway of armed guards. Paxton stood aside waiting to collect his earnings for the night. She had not been his only sale, but the other woman had appeared blessedly incoherent. Forward, she faced the eyes of a hundred dark predators, staring, eager for conquest. She couldn't breathe without tasting their steamy, musky sweat. Finally, to her right, stairs to a place she didn't want to know about. The place they took the slaves. Her stomach wrenched with dread.

Panic hit hard and fast.

She woke up from her temporary daze and leapt. Unfortunately, the arm encircling her neck caught and tightened. Turning her head sideways inside his grip, Alex bit hard into the salty, hairy flesh. Disgusting, but effective.

A remarkably high-pitched yelp rewarded her efforts

before the air at her throat was cut off. Her vision blurred, and her body trembled. The guard gave an inch. She hissed in a sharp breath. The second she regained her focus and footing she spat, "Obviously, your mother didn't teach you any manners, you stinking, filthy, brainless bastard."

She croaked more than cursed, but the slurs felt good nonetheless.

Alex regretted the outburst immediately when a murmur of curiosity, expectation, then appreciation, spread across the room. As if her struggle excited them. Her eyes burned with terror. God help her. They were all animals.

Joshua Leigh looked up at the commotion. He'd been having an exceptional night out with his friends—until now. Right now, he felt sick. His cohorts thought to impress him with admittance to one of the special markets—a Moroccan slave auction. To the buyers, a very civil affair. To the slaves, the beginning of a nightmare.

Joshua raked a hand through his hair, yearning for escape. They had missed most of "the evening's highlights," and thankfully the experience was nearly over.

He surveyed the small square room, crammed with lustful buyers, and suffused in cigar smoke. Although he was in the back, his height gave him a clear view of the makeshift auction block and the buyers eager to make a purchase. They no doubt had experienced every known pleasure and out of boredom sought more. There was no thought of moral consequences. When you were this rich you could control the consequences.

A howl from the barrel-chested guard escorting the

current captive caught his attention. The girl choked on a scream, her long braid coming undone, and spilling rich, auburn tresses over her shoulders. A buzz began in the room. Joshua tensed, watching the girl struggle in vain against the enormous creature twice her size.

Witnessing her vulnerability, he was forced to think of his own. Of everything he had worked and sweat for in the last four years. He was making a life for himself. An honest one. One that had nothing to do with his bastard father, and nothing to do with this. His current shipment would put him in the black. If he delivered it on time.

Why then, would the thought of losing it all even come into consideration?

He quickly assessed the possible exits, as was his habit in a tricky negotiation. The trading business was oftentimes dangerous and he knew from experience when to walk away before it got messy.

Every rational thought told him to walk away now.

He looked at the girl again, and sighed regretfully, stepping backward to blend more into his surroundings.

Alex continued to look out, not sparing anyone her disdain. If she could remember their faces it would give her focus in the days to come. She fully intended to kill every one of them. In this lifetime. For now, she must face reality and find a way to survive. She was a Stafford after all. She would survive. Somehow, she prayed, she would survive.

Alex cursed every man in Morocco, and then herself for wanting to come here. This trip had been a chance to prove herself. Her first voyage as the youngest captain for

Stafford Shipping. True, she had been accompanied by her father's and brothers' ships, but at sea she'd been in charge.

This last month had been all she ever imagined. Of course, many parts of Morocco were crowded, dirty, and dangerous. Her father didn't trust her to go anywhere alone. After the humiliation of being kidnapped, she grudgingly admitted he might be right. If she survived, this current setback could last years. That thought alone was abysmally depressing. She would be forever proving herself.

She licked her lips, parched and desperate for one drop of water. Deep weariness made every limb seem twice its weight. Even her hands ached from the guard's tight hold. Undoubtedly, he had ceased the blood flow to her fingers. Hopelessness caused a burning sensation in her eyes, and her head wilted causing wild strands of hair to stick to her cheeks. She wanted to give up.

A man came up to her, his personal odor preceding him. She saw only feet and some flowing robes. He was a potential customer, and Alex understood clearly his command that she look up. She also considered it fair enough that she was not in the mood to cooperate.

The buyer was smug and undeterred. He grasped her chin in demand. To be relieved of his touch, she gave in and forced herself to gaze past his stout body. She recognized the words of appreciation as well as the scrutiny up and down meant to denigrate.

Defiance disappeared as she smiled tentatively, forcing herself to look him in the eyes. He froze, surprised, then grinned oafishly. Alex felt not an ounce of remorse at his disconcerted look. If he was that stupid, he deserved what he got.

He was still smiling dimwittedly when the shin of Alex's leg connected with his groin. The guard immediately pulled her back. Using the hold from behind as leverage, Alex jumped up, lifting both her legs, and pushed the man off the stage. There was a gratifying thump. A rush of satisfaction gave her new strength.

The fallen man got up with a murderous look. Joshua started instinctively, then stopped. He needn't have worried. The "goods" were well protected and the humiliated buyer escorted aside amid laughter and lusty admiration.

His stomach twisted again as the girl straightened her back and lifted her head. Her eyes sparkled clear and pure, and her hair was the color of rich cherry wood with a warmth and texture that lured him, even through the dirty haze of smoke. She was young, which might account for her somewhat strange clothing—a tailored shirt, that could have been designed for a man, was torn at the throat, revealing more than it was meant to. Her skirt was not a skirt, but loose gentleman's pants that must have been made to order. A large belt cinched them at her waist with a decorative buckle. They were some kind of work clothes, but for what profession he knew not. From the surprisingly strong voice that spit out at the room in Arabic, he'd mark her as a survivor. That, at least, was a good sign.

"You will all rot in bloody hell, and I promise to send

each one of you foul, pathetic, immoral scum there myself."

Joshua winced. There were a few guffaws from the locals. Educated, but obviously not the daughter of a diplomat. The girl then added what curses and slurs she seemed able to summon in Spanish, French, Italian, the local dialect, and what he thought might be Chinese. No, he decided recognizing some of the words, definitely no diplomats in the family. A resounding slap echoed in his ears as she was struck across the face, her head snapping, stunning her into temporary silence.

A ferocious rage struck him just as quickly, and his friend grabbed his arm in warning. He swallowed impatience, fighting for control, and found himself urging her on. Praying she could magically absorb a little of his strength to survive her torment.

The next seconds seemed like hours as he waited to see if she would recover from the blow, uncertain she was not already unconscious. Then, very slowly, with painstaking control, she lifted her chin. A clenched jaw, made the angles of her face even sharper, and he sensed her strength to move came only from blood-sizzling fury and sheer determination. He stepped back unconsciously at the fire in her eyes and watched with admiration as she returned the strike with one of her own.

She spat.

He guessed she had decent aim when the Moroccan wiped a slow hand across his chin and mouth. He raised his arm again threateningly, but she refused to cower. She did make the concession of keeping her mouth shut. For that, Joshua was relieved. Most of the men likely didn't understand her threats and slurs against their manhood, but the way her lips curled with disgust conveyed the meaning as well as any word. She was haughty as a queen, yet he knew she was frightened. Hell, if she wasn't, then she was downright stupid.

The guard wrenched her arms from behind and earned a sharp flinch from his captive. It was an act of brutality merely for the pleasure of it. Joshua had experienced it often as a boy, and empathy twisted his guts at the memory. He acknowledged then what he had known the instant he'd seen her—she was doomed, and somehow, God help him, he had to save her.

What a damned mess.

There was an intimate description of the goods before the bidding took off feverishly.

It stopped when a bid from the side won silence. Joshua recognized the round, middle-aged sultan who had just doubled the last offer. The man was richer than any king in Europe and known to keep harems in each of his many palaces. He was also known for a cruel streak in ruling his people. He would no doubt take great pleasure in breaking this girl of her spirit.

Throwing caution to the wind, Joshua stepped forward and raised the bid. He had no idea how he would get his hands on that kind of money, but he didn't care.

There was a collective murmur of shock in the room. Not because of the costly price he realized, but because he dared to bid against the sultan.

The sultan bid again, but Joshua voiced a higher price, heedless of his own increasing peril.

The sultan then offered a small fortune, and the bidding ended.

Joshua watched the girl curse and fight as they dragged her off the stage to the other side of the platform. His blood burned. All the injustices he had ever experienced came to a head. He couldn't bear to see another innocent creature ruined by the egos and will of greedy men.

"It is over, my friend. Let's go." His companion, the sultan's nephew, pulled his arm urgently.

"Where are they taking her?"

"There are quarters upstairs," Prince Raja explained. "Al-Aziz gets her only for tonight. She is not allowed to leave the rooms here. He paid well to be the first. Soon there will be another auction. A rare piece like that will bring them much money." The prince read his friend's expression. "Please, my friend, do not do anything foolish."

Joshua's lips curved slightly. "Me?"

Raja sighed, "I cannot be involved. I am easily recognized and my cousin is my responsibility."

Joshua recalled his cousin was currently laid out drunk in Raja's carriage.

"But…if you live long enough," Raja hesitated then whispered some directions indicating a meeting place on the edge of the city. "They will expect you to go where it is busy. Do not. I will find you." He paused with warning. "If that is still an option."

Joshua gripped Raja's hand gratefully.

The prince rebuked, "Do not thank me. I should have never brought you here."

Joshua watched as the auctioneer paid the slave trader, then turned back to Raja, grinning. "It was fate, my friend. Fear not."

Alex cursed as Paxton collected an obscene amount of gold. It was entirely unjust. He lifted it toward her in a salute then handed it to a companion while a new guard undid her bounds. Paxton wasn't more than fourteen feet away. She could kill him. With a knife. Perhaps the one being used to free her. It had cut through the ropes efficiently enough. But then she had to reach him. Too many people moving about. Not a direct throw.

Not to worry.

Saying words of thanks in Arabic to the guard who freed her, she turned around and added a respectful nod. The guard looked into her eyes. She smiled—for good measure—distracting him. Two seconds later she had the knife. Four seconds later she was in striking distance of Paxton.

Paxton didn't anticipate trouble coming his way. He turned at the sudden noise. Not expecting her. Not expecting the shadow of a knife to flash before him.

In range, Alex leaped, triumph in her last breath.

Someone caught her ankle.

She stretched, determined, victory near. Her target clear.

Paxton's eyes made contact with hers.

She reached for his throat.

And missed.

Paxton turned his head away defensively as she struck. Blood spurted free as the knife opened skin down the side of his left cheek. He cried in rage as Alex fell forward to the ground, several guards instantly on her, a foot crushing her knife-wielding hand. Paxton tried to get at her in the fray, seeking revenge but was held back.

Someone gave him a rag. Held apart, he faced her as she was lifted to her feet, a look of pure evil burning in his eyes. "You will live to regret this, Stafford."

"Not," she gasped, being pulled away, "while there is a breath left in my body!"

Paxton's face contorted into something monstrous. "Then start counting your days."

<br>

Get the rest of the story at Amazon.com
or TrishAlbright.com

**Excerpt from**

**SIREN'S SECRET**

## CHAPTER ONE

*London, 1791*

Lady Olivia Katharine Hastings Yates, known for her exemplary standards, excellent taste, and exceptional mind, was about to become a thief.

She stared at the artifact before her. Her fingertips tingled, her senses heightened, and her life was about to change forever.

But what choice was there?

She picked up the ancient Egyptian funerary cone, instantly disgusted.

"They really should improve the security here." This *was* the British Museum. Home to countless priceless artifacts! One less artifact now.

Olivia ignored the fact that her first bit of thieving left very little remorse. It was actually a bit thrilling, if she was honest. And surprisingly easy. Completely wrong, but *most* exciting, all in all. She sighed, relieved she'd been able to succeed. Her jaw relaxed a moment.

One step closer to saving her father.

A chilling waft of air struck her, and Olivia realized a window was open somewhere. That could not be safe either. She would be sure to tell Grayson they needed to check their security.

She glanced around Grayson's dark research room, lifting her lamp past the tables of books and artifacts being studied. The windows appeared closed.

*Strange.*

Olivia brushed away any worries, her attention returning to the artifact.

She lifted it carefully, weighing. Solid red granite. Heavier than expected. Another thrill went through her— this one entirely academic. She was holding an item more than two thousand years old. She reverently traced the ancient hieroglyphics engraved on the rounded end, recognizing instantly many words she had already translated, and studying new ones, her mind racing with excitement, a strange familiarity and understanding rushing her.

Turning it over, she observed how the stone narrowed into the shape of a five-pointed star on the other end—as if designed for a secondary purpose, perhaps to hold the marker in place.

"Unusual," she murmured. She didn't recognize the strange symbol chiseled inside the star either. It didn't look Egyptian, but according to the writing, this funerary cone marked the resting place of a librarian at the Great Library of Alexandria. She touched the symbol.

Her head spun, and she put the ancient object down for safety.

The sensation stopped.

*Odd. The excitement, no doubt.*

Olivia took a breath. It was time to go. She needed to walk out of the room, smile pleasantly, compliment Grayson and the other hosts, then leave the fund-raising event as quickly as possible.

Her eyes darted around the room for anything else of value she should snatch while she had the chance. If she was joining the profession, she intended to be good at it.

On the desk, not far from where the artifact had been, was a paper. She recognized Lord Grayson's exacting script.

He had noted all the symbols of the funerary cone, with special care to possible meanings underneath, but was completely wrong in his theory.

"Not even close, dear Grayson," Olivia said softly.

There was also an inscription included from where the stone had been acquired. The hieroglyphics struck her with sudden clarity. *What you seek, you already have.*

Olivia's head spun again. She braced herself against the table.

Touching the ancient stone, Olivia was more certain than ever that she had the code for translating hieroglyphics correct. Only no one believed her.

Why would they? She had not attended Eton, Oxford, or any institution of note. After all, she was a woman. Her entire education had been achieved through private tutors and her father's library. Fortunately, her father had one of the largest personal libraries in London. But, oh, to one day speak at the very institutions she was barred from and share her knowledge. To exchange ideas with other great minds. She knew it was improbable, but she dreamed…someday.

This artifact might be the key.

Aside from the stealing part. That could become an issue.

Her father's colleague in Egypt had sent this to the British Museum in hope that Grayson and others could decipher the notable Alexandrian's text.

She folded the paper and shoved it deep into the pocket of her gown. A creaking sound at the far end of the room sent a shot of ice down her arms. She whirled and stared into blackness.

Nothing.

Bookcases settling, no doubt, but a reminder that she needed to make her departure.

She tucked the Egyptian relic into the crook of her elbow, concealed it with her thick cloak, and pressed it snug against her body. Next she covered the wick of the lamp until darkness enveloped her, save for the moonlight through the window, and made for the door.

That's when the creak turned to a scuttle. A fast scuttle. Little hairs on the back of her neck prickled. She turned defensively as a large shadow moved across the room.

Straight at her.

She rushed toward the light illuminating the crack under the door.

Something caught at her throat and pulled her backward, choking. The granite cone slipped from her grasp and fell with a muffled thud before hitting the wood floor. A man yelped. She realized the stone must have landed strategically, giving her a moment's reprieve. She turned and swung wildly, furiously, flinching when her weak fist made contact with something that felt like a chin.

"Bastard!" she spat, furious at her injured hand.

He ripped her cloak from her tangled grasp and threw it over her head, causing not just utter darkness, but *suffocating* utter darkness. Olivia struggled in earnest, crying out for help, her voice effectively muffled in velvet and mink, her head getting hot, her thoughts becoming fuzzy, her hair ruined for sure, but worse—she was being carried toward the windows.

She should have known stealing wouldn't be this easy. Despite all her planning, there were things in the world of thieving she hadn't taken into account.

Other thieves.

Samuel Stafford accepted the sealed message from Lord Grayson, promising to deliver it when he arrived in Alexandria. Egypt was an occasional port of call for him on his Mediterranean route for Stafford Shipping, and often families and business associates asked him to carry correspondence.

"Thank you, Stafford. I appreciate your assistance. There aren't many ships journeying so far at this time. And there are few non-English vessels known to be so successful in avoiding pirates these days." Grayson added, curious, "I've heard it is a family secret?"

Samuel smiled politely. With America unwilling to pay off the Barbary States, few of its ships could count on safe passage after the war with England. Fortunately, his parents had laid the groundwork for secure routes through the Mediterranean. But he didn't share family adventures with mere acquaintances, so he responded vaguely. "We have been lucky."

Grayson nodded, accepting the answer. "If you see the duchess, please give her my regards," Grayson added.

"The duchess?"

"Your sister, Mr. Stafford." The wiry Englishman grinned.

Samuel still had a hard time remembering his wild little sister had an English title. It was so…un-American.

Grayson continued, "She visited before her departure, wanting to borrow a book on Egyptian myths. I understand she'll be visiting some of the sights in Egypt, and she thought it would be enriching." He indicated the correspondence. "Lord Merryvale offered her a tour around his current excavation site as well."

Samuel nodded. "She is an avid reader. It passes the hours at sea. I'll be certain to share your greeting."

"Excellent. Please enjoy the rest of the evening, then."

Samuel looked around at the emptiness of the second-floor exhibit rooms set up for the occasion. They had been given the grand tour earlier, and now the guests happily congregated where music played and champagne flowed. He liked silence. One would think he got enough of it at sea, but London was at times overwhelming, with the sheer number of people in the city.

"Mind if I stay a bit?" he asked. "I could use a moment from the crowd."

"Of course," Grayson replied. "All the second-floor rooms are open in this wing. The third floor is off-limits, but nothing to be missed. Office and study space mostly."

Samuel waited as the man bowed and excused himself. Once alone, he strolled the open space, making his way through a couple more rooms, enjoying the opportunity to browse at his leisure. It was peaceful, save for the light hum of revelers wafting up from the bottom floor. He didn't care much for Greek vases, but he wholeheartedly supported the intent of the museum to give free entry to all who wished to look at them and other antiquities they had begun to collect.

Few of the very rich downstairs seemed genuinely interested in the history marked on each table, but they appreciated the endeavor with their pocket funds.

He rolled his shoulders under his coat, wishing for fresh air, when something at the window caught his eye. He blinked, curious.

A pair of feet?

Samuel stepped closer to the window, the light from inside illuminating the vision. Suddenly the feet dropped, and a pair of stocking-covered legs hung, swinging, searching for purchase. It took him less than a second to realize this was a stunning pair of legs. Even less to realize a woman was hanging outside, in danger of losing her life.

He opened the window to save her from certain death and reached up to grasp what was both a distracting and rather luscious view—when the unthinkable happened.

A leg swung fiercely forward, its foot leading the strike on his face with enough force to knock him backward and temporarily blind him.

Olivia struggled furiously against her captor. Gads. Not just a thief, but a murdering thief. He intended to toss her out the window! She was going to die—and not nobly. Instead, she'd be remembered for a notorious and mysterious death, discussed in hush tones among the ton for years to come.

She felt a blast of cold air up her legs as she kicked hard, hoping for a wall or windowpane to use as leverage against being forced out.

"Hurry. Someone's coming."

Olivia renewed her muffled screams at the new voice, hoping against hope someone would arrive in time. She would worry about explanations later.

Unfortunately, it was not to be done.

An icy breeze rushed up her skirts as her body was lifted and pushed feet first through the third-floor window.

The word *crushing* went through her mind. *A crushing fall,* they would all say.

Then outrage took over. She would not be easily finished. Her father needed her, and she was all he had. And he, all *she* had. No, this would not do.

Olivia clawed frantically, managing to free a hand from the heavy cloak. She swiped at her attacker, grasping hold near his collar as he tried to toss her. Something ripped, but she clung. Then her body dropped, weightless, the cloak finally freeing itself.

She fell.

For a full second.

Then jolted to a stop.

Olivia clung to silk neckwear, listening with satisfaction to the choking sounds of her attacker. Her other hand fumbled free and scraped against the cold wall searching for hope. It came in contact with what she knew to be vines.

That's when the weight of her attacker shifted. She wrenched her neck sideways to see where he would attack from next, and suddenly he was coming down.

On top of her.

Olivia gladly released him, and swung to the side of the wall clinging to vines on pure faith.

Her attacker suffered worse misfortune. He crashed headfirst. She shuddered at the crush. *That* was a crushing death.

She tilted her head toward the window hoping help was within reach. Instead the window shut emphatically, leaving her to contemplate her lack of botanical knowledge regarding vines. She prayed these were the sturdy sort.

The vines ripped.

In a desperate moment, with a desperate cry, she reached with her left hand to a small ledge dividing the floors while scooping her right hand around another fresh set of vines. She hung perilously.

Until those vines ripped too. Her body jolted lower.

Olivia breathed deep and slow, holding back a whimper of fear. Below her was light. Another window. Maybe she could swing in—except her arms ached, her fingers burned raw, and her heart pounded so hard she had trouble making her legs function. She hung, clinging to the vines, unable to commit to either plant or stone. What were the odds the window was open? It was early spring—too cold for open windows. If she moved too violently she might lose her already hazardous hold on life.

She was doomed. Her thieving days over for certain.

Olivia decided risk was the only option. She swung a leg, thinking to crack the glass.

Luck! It was open.

Bad luck. The vines ripped.

She yelped, skidding against the building until her foot landed with a jolt on a narrow ledge. Her heart thundered in her ears and dizziness threatened. She was parallel to the window. A mere foot from safety.

Carefully Olivia inched her body toward the light, uncaring that her dress was bunched, her hands raw, and her hair falling free. She just…needed…to reach…the window.

One arm reached toward the opening, her fingers scraping along cold stone toward the heat of the room.

She felt the vine weakening and released, making a grab for the windowpane. Painstakingly, she shimmied inch by inch across the ledge. She could have cried with joy when she finally hugged the window frame with her body. With one neat sidestep she prepared to jump inside.

That's when she made the biggest mistake of her life.

She looked up.

And saw him.

A giant. A monster. A brute of a man. Inches away. Reaching for her!

In fright, she gasped. And made an even bigger mistake.

She let go.


Get the rest of the story soon on Amazon.com

Or TrishAlbright.com

**Excerpt from**

## SIREN'S SANCTUARY

## CHAPTER ONE

*1792, England…nearly*

The blind seer. That's what they called her in Macau. When they really wished to mock her, they would say: blind seer, daughter of the sea goddess, afraid of the sea. A useless coward.

*And all of it true.*

Luli closed her eyes, eyes that worked perfectly, and hoped for a vision that would guide her through this terrible moment and give her courage.

At the sound of cannon blast, she squeezed them tighter, breathing rhythmically, and moved her body through formation. Her Taijiquan practice was the one thing that kept her sane. Despite her profound fear of the sea, it kept her calm. Storms, illness, Canton pirates, Dutch pirates, even worse—the town matchmaker—Luli had weathered them all without complaint. The ancient movements gave her peace. They were the only thing still familiar in her world other than Uncle Bing and Min Ming.

Her body stumbled, then, as was necessary at the thought of Min Ming, she took four more breaths until she felt serenity enter her mind and body again.

Min Ming, with her constant criticisms and demands issued in high-pitched nasal lamentations, had shared with Luli the same eight square feet for eleven months, twenty-five days, three hours and ten minutes. That's how long they had been traveling. Had Luli known her fate, she might have waited for another vision—or brought a sleeping potion.

She smoothly turned in the small space, keeping balance on one foot and landing low.

She opened one eye again, and smiled briefly, imagining 'fig face' going to sleep at Luli's command.

That was the gift Luli would have asked for—not visions.

Her breath hitched at the thought. Not that she had much experience even with visions. She'd only had one, nearly a year ago. And look at the mess now. Uncle's gentle questions the last months made her think even he believed she had misinterpreted the vision. But she had not asked Uncle Bing or Min Ming to come with her. That had been their choice. Thankfully, her uncle had insisted. He had saved them more than once the last year, his ability to understand the human heart guiding them toward good people and away from bad ones. Min Ming seemed the only anomaly to that truth.

Another blast sounded, followed by the splintering

explosion of wood. A tingle of fear shot up the back of her neck. That one hit. The English Navy longer merely warned them. She rubbed her palms against her worn tunic, and continued her practice fighting now to keep frustration and anger out of her heart.

Crashing waves, cannon fire, sea monsters, and long torturous hours of Min Ming's lectures expounding on everything that was wrong with her, could have made another person throw themselves to their death in the icy waves. But she—Lucia Leonore Luli Da Costa, daughter on Wei Meili, of Shen Wu, of Lang Su, great-great granddaughter of Ling Li Shan, who saved Yinzhen, the royal son of His Imperial Majesty, Emporer Kangxi—had remained calm.

*Calm*!

She inhaled a controlled breath and released.

Now, her destination in sight, this England, this foreign place that she sailed around the world for, out of duty to generations of ancestors, to fulfill the sacrifice her mother and those before her had made—this England—would not let them enter.

Even worse, their navy fired cannons at them!

Luli trembled as she glided through practiced moves of taijiquan, focusing her *qi*. *Cross arms. Wrest tiger.*

She would remain *calm*.

The sound of her cabin door spinning back to crash into the wall interrupted that calm.

Min Ming burst into the small room and stood there in the doorway, brown, wrinkled, and diminutive. She waited for Luli to acknowledge her.

Luli nodded her head respectfully then closed her eyes against the scrunched up scowl that made the old woman look like an angry fig. A dried, angry fig face. Then she berated herself for disrespectful thoughts. Ming suffered as well. The journey had not been easy for anyone. Another cannon shook the vessel. She opened her eyes, alert, gliding into the next form with determination. *Drag a monkey. Sink needle to sea.*

"Ship here!" Min Ming said in English.

*Stretch back like fan.* "What's happening?" Luli asked.

"Listen! Ship here!"

When Luli continued to move into the next pose, Min Ming scurried to Luli's small silk hip bag in the top drawer of the bolted down chest.

Luli's mind connected when the old woman opened Luli's bag and pulled out the folded parchment she'd been carrying around for eleven months, twenty-five days, three hours and fourteen minutes.

She pulled her limbs into an upright position. "That ship?" she asked, staring at the drawing, incredulous.

Relief, disbelief, and worry clashed in her mind erasing every sense of calm for which she'd labored. She had been traveling for nearly a year to find this ship. It was her first clue—the key to her duty.

And now it was here?

"Yes, yes. Your ship! And now, maybe it will save us...or kill us."

"What is happening?" Luli maintained her tree pose,

breathing slowly for patience.

Longer explanations required words she'd yet to master so Min Ming explained in a mix of Cantonese, Portuguese and English. "Captain say English want the cargo. Your ship is behind us. Pirates maybe. They want cargo too. Don't know." Ming gathered her things. "I saw cannon hit us. Ship is going to sink. Everybody die. Your fault."

Luli remained silent. There wasn't much she could say to that. It was always her fault. And since they were here, at this exact moment in time because of her, Luli could not fault anyone else.

"Where's my uncle?"

"On deck. Hit. Laying down to die."

"What?" Luli's energy exploded throughout the room more powerfully then intended. Then all the pent of fear she sought to control engulfed her. Her heart pounded and her breath hitched painfully for air.

Ming jumped. Then shouted back. "You get what you deserve now! Always disrespectful. No surprise no one wanted you. Too big, too fat, too disrespectful."

Luli sucked for air again, humiliated at the truth and straining for control. "I'm sorry."

"Maybe not so bad. Wei Bing very stubborn." Then Min Ming smiled at her—knowingly. "Go see." She waited, "Before your ship sail away, and uncle die, and you are failure. Hurry, go up." She waved to the open passageway, the door swinging back and forth dangerously.

Luli trembled, her feet sticking to the floor in fear. *Mean old fig face.*

Min Ming laughed at her frozen feet. "Ha, ha. Daughter of Meili have no courage."

"I do." Luli forced one foot to lift. It landed hard not far from where it started. She tried the other one, with an inch more of success. "The ship is not going to sink. I will find Uncle."

Ming hopped on the bed and folded her hands on her lap entertained. "I watch."

Luli swallowed the lump in her throat and move her right foot again. Closer this time.

Ming cackled and slapped the bed with one hand, her amusement complete.

Luli felt her eyes burn but forced her emotion aside.

The second cackle spurred her on, if for nothing else than to protect her mother's good name. But there was more. Uncle Bing was her only living relative. He had sheltered her for three years, before leaving his home, his country, and his business to follow her. She would never let anything happen to him.

Luli finally caught the door and gritted her teeth. Her confidence plummeted once again. Min Ming, for all her faults, was right. She had no courage. Not when it came to water.

Except for their few stops on land, she'd traveled for a year staying primarily in a space only big enough for a bed, a chair and two people to stand.

"Hurry. Your uncle will be dead before you get there!" Another cackle started then turned into a choked, hacking cough.

"I am Lucia—" The ship rocked unnaturally and another crashing sound of lead through wood vibrated around her. Luli squeaked in panic as she threw the door open and pressed her back to wall outside. The gangplank to the upper deck was to her left. Slowly she sidestepped against the wall until she reached the narrow steps at the end. "I am Lucia Leonore Da Costa—" Luli looked up as a shadow blocked light.

Then it came tumbling toward her.

She jumped back, but not in time. A sailor landed at her feet, his body crushing her toes and trapping her against the wall. She hated herself for welcoming an excuse to not go on, before wiggling each foot free. The injured sailor helped when he rolled onto his side, moaning.

Blood seeped through his fingers where he touched the injury.

Instantly concerned, Luli tried to aid him. "I'm fine. Just a little blood," he said.

"I'll get help." And though it was selfish to ask, she did anyway. "Have you seen my uncle?"

"On deck…"

"I'll return." Luli lunged for the sloped ladder in front of her and took the first step up the gangway.

"Hurry," he urged.

"I will." Forcing her hand to release one step and grip another took intense focus. "Yes. I'll return," she said again.

A moment later the sailor mumbled in a tone that made her think he was not convinced. "You're still here."

She should have been insulted. She was from a long line of heroic women.

She lifted her hand again and gripped the last step of the ladder, any false confidence she harbored, disappearing in suffocating terror. Feeling light-headed, she breathed deeply in and out. Puffy gray clouds filled the sky. She took another step and poked her head out, forcing an exhale. "Don't look past the ship." If she could stay focused, it would be fine. "Head down."

It didn't work.

The ship wasn't big enough to block her views. All around, they were surrounded by water. *A vast, dark, forbidding ocean.*

Land was not far off. The England. Two other vessels stalked them on either side—one firing, the other trapping them, ready to board. *Her ship.* The vision was real. Instead of savoring the victory, she closed her eyes with disappointment. It seemed they wanted to steal from them too. That's all anybody did.

When Luli opened her eyes again, she saw her uncle. He leaned against the side of the ship, furthest from the action.

And furthest from her.

Seeing him struck down filled her with a greater terror than water. Without thinking, Luli hurried toward him, careful to duck lines, and swinging sails, and avoid the dazed sailor that nearly knocked her over. She stopped a moment to find air, her heart pounding so hard she thought it might explode from her chest. *Must remain calm.*

The Captain stood at the rail near Uncle Bing, yelling

across to the new ship. She held onto the hope they were friendly, as they did not appear ready for attack. But they sailed closer. So close she thought they would crash.

They didn't.

Instead, the ship floated by and three men swung from the short distance between ships, landing on the decks in front of her.

Only, they were not just men.

They were giants.

Anyone in Macau who thought her five foot two frame was tall, would pick a new description if she was standing next to them. They were three times Min Ming's height! Temporarily distracted she kept her eyes on them and wove her way that direction, toward the giants, and toward her uncle. One of them bent to her uncle. Luli moved faster, ready to protect Uncle Bing. Nearly there, she swayed left to keep balance then righted herself with the ship, before sliding down on her knees and taking her uncle's hand in panic. There was a large knot on his forehead.

The words flowed between them as he reassured her he would live.

Completely unaware that anyone but her uncle could understand their Macanese dialect, she bemoaned the situation. "This is all my fault."

A deep, smooth voice questioned her guilt. "You made the British Navy fire on you, miss?"

The words were in English, but in response to her Cantonese. Startled, she followed a long tanned arm up to the face of the owner.

Then, after eleven months and twenty-six days, three hours and twenty-eight minutes—Luli found the man she must save.

Get the rest of the story soon on Amazon.com
Or TrishAlbright.com

www.ingramcontent.com/pod-product-compliance
Lightning Source LLC
Chambersburg PA
CBHW060820120626
46557CB00001B/293